Tangled Up With You

A SMALL TOWN SURPRISE PREGNANCY ROMANCE

SECOND HOPE SERIES

JESSICA PRINCE

This book is for the wild child in every one of us.
We might have made questionable decisions in our lifetime,
but at least we have some entertaining stories to tell.

Let's Connect

Let's Connect

By signing up for my newsletter, you're guaranteeing you'll stay up to date on all new releases, cover reveals, giveaways, sales, and all the other exciting book news I have coming!

I pinky-promise to use my emails for good only, not to spam you, and make sure each one is enjoyable for everybody.

Sign up on my website at:

www.authorjessicaprince.com

If you're curious about where Connor and Ivy got their starts, I've attached a little graphic below to make that easier for you.

I hope you enjoy this story as much as I enjoyed writing it!

Happy reading, and all the love,
~ Jess

Discover Other Books by Jessica

SECOND HOPE SERIES
The Little Things
Tangled Up With You

ASHLAND SERIES
Dead to Rights

WHITECAP SERIES
Crossing the Line
My Perfect Enemy
Turn of the Tides

THE PEMBROOKE SERIES:
Sweet Sunshine
Coming Full Circle

A Broken Soul
Should Have Been Me

<u>WHISKEY DOLLS SERIES</u>
Bombshell
Knockout
Stunner
Seductress
Temptress
Vamp

<u>HOPE VALLEY SERIES:</u>
Out of My League
Come Back Home Again
The Best of Me
Wrong Side of the Tracks
Stay With Me
Out of the Darkness
The Second Time Around
Waiting for Forever
Love to Hate You
Playing for Keeps
When You Least Expect It
Never for Him

<u>REDEMPTION SERIES</u>

Bad Alibi
Crazy Beautiful
Bittersweet
Guilty Pleasure
Wallflower
Blurred Line
Slow Burn
Favorite Mistake
Sweet Spot

THE CLOVERLEAF SERIES
Picking up the Pieces
Rising from the Ashes
Pushing the Boundaries
Worth the Wait

THE COLORS NOVELS
Scattered Colors
Shrinking Violet
Love Hate Relationship
Wildflower

THE LOCKLAINE BOYS
Fire & Ice
Opposites Attract
Almost Perfect

<u>CIVIL CORRUPTION SERIES</u>

Corrupt
Defile
Consume
Ravage

<u>GIRL TALK SERIES:</u>

Seducing Lola
Tempting Sophia
Enticing Daphne
Charming Fiona

<u>STANDALONE TITLES:</u>

One Knight Stand
Chance Encounters
Nightmares from Within

<u>DEADLY LOVE SERIES:</u>

Destructive
Addictive

"The Fire" by Chris Stapleton
"White Horse" by Chris Stapleton
"Something in the Orange" by Zach Bryan
"I Don't Remember Me" by Brothers Osborne
"Sun to Me" by Zach Bryan
"Crosswind" by Chris Stapleton
"Stick Season" by Noah Kahan
"Dial Drunk" by Noah Kahan and Post Malone
"Who's Afraid of Little Old Me" by Taylor Swift
"Nightmare" by Halsey
"Fortnight" by Taylor Swift feat. Post Malone

Chapter One

CONNOR

The ice cubes in my glass clinked against the sides as I brought it to my lips and drank deep. The whiskey left a trail of heat down my throat before the biting, smokey flavor settled in my stomach and spread outward, warming me from the inside, like I was sitting in front of a campfire. I usually stuck to beer when I was riding, but that wasn't going to cut it tonight. Not if I wanted to take the edge off the tension that had my muscles bunched into knots and numb the pain in my knee.

I felt it as soon as I launched off that bull earlier. The damn thing had finally healed up enough for me to get back to work, but now I couldn't stop worrying that I'd fucked it up all over again and what that could mean for my future.

I'd had a good ride. A hell of a ride, actually—best of the night. I came in first, getting me that much closer to the World Championships. But as soon as the buzzer sounded and I jumped off the rank bastard I'd pulled for tonight's ride, I hit the dirt of that arena in a way that sent a lightning bolt of pain from my knee all the way up into my hip. It had nearly been enough to knock the breath from my lungs and take me to the ground. The only thing that kept me standing and moving was the seventeen hundred pounds of pissed-off animal gunning for me, and I needed to get my ass out of the way.

I played down the pain as best I could, pinning my signature smile to my face as I pulled my hat off and waved it at the cheering crowd. I assured the trainers nothing was wrong, but the goddamn thing hadn't stopped throbbing in the hours since. It had taken an act of pure will to keep my back straight and my stride even when all I wanted to do was beg to have my ass wheeled out of the arena in a wheelchair, and now I was trying to dull the ache with booze and over-the-counter pain meds that I'd been crunching on like Sweet Tarts all damn night.

I was tired. Christ, I was so damn tired. I felt beat to hell. The older I got, the more my body felt every single effect of those bulls thrashing me around like I was a rag doll. I was only thirty-four, for fuck's sake, but lately I'd been feeling a hell of a lot older. It was taking longer and longer to work the stiffness out of my muscles when I woke up every morning. Hell, it took me a good two or three minutes to limp my ass to the bathroom like a goddamn octogenarian just to take a piss after rolling out of bed.

Shameful.

But it wasn't just physical exhaustion that had been weighing my shoulders down the past few months. I was drained mentally as well. I used to live for this shit. All I cared about was riding bulls, getting laid, and raising a little hell along the way—in that order. I wanted to make a name for myself, to win it all and be known as the best bull rider of my time, and I wanted to have a hell of a lot of fun while doing it.

Now it all just felt . . . empty. Hard as I might try, I hadn't been able to find the joy in any of it lately. Going out and tying a few on after a good ride, or finding something soft, warm, and wet to bury my cock in to celebrate just didn't hold the same appeal it used to. The adrenaline high of riding was still there, but it wore off a lot faster than it had in the past. This used to be my sole reason for existing. I used to love spending my nights after a hell of a ride drinking and fucking just to wake up the next day and do it all over again, climb my reckless ass onto the back of another bull to show the crowd how good I was at it. But now . . . Christ, it was painful to admit, but I was bored. Even . . . lonely.

Something had changed. And as much as I wanted to deny it, I knew exactly when it happened. How it happened.

It was all *her* fault.

Ivy Young.

That sweet, tempting she-devil with the pale red hair, a wild streak a mile wide, and curves that would tempt a saint.

She sank her claws into me a few months back and hadn't let go.

Well, that wasn't really fair. I mean, I was just as complicit in everything that had happened between us as she was. Maybe even more so. But she wasn't supposed to have been able to burrow her way beneath my skin as deeply as she had. I had my guards up to prevent that very thing from ever happening. A large, fortified, electric fence surrounded by a piranha-infested moat a mile wide.

I'd learned my lesson the hard way to stay as far away from those kinds of feelings as possible. I knew firsthand they only led to heartache, yet that little minx was well and truly stuck in my head. I couldn't remember a day in the past few months when I hadn't thought about her at least once an hour.

I first laid eyes on Ivy when I showed up in Hope

Valley several months back. I'd been forced to take a break after busting up my knee. I went back to Cloverleaf, the small Texas town where I'd grown up, to see my parents and started rehabbing my knee, but it didn't take long for me to go stir-crazy. I had two choices: I could stay in Cloverleaf and get lost in the bottom of a bottle, drinking away my boredom and the self-pity I was suffering through from not being able to ride bulls, or I could pack my stuff and hit the road.

I chose the safer option, deciding to go visit my buddy Zach on his ranch in Virginia. I'd been there a few times before and had always liked the little town's vibe. There was just something about it that stood out to me—made it special. Cloverleaf would always hold a special place in my heart. It was where I'd been born and raised, my whole family was still there, all the friends I'd grown up with. But there was something about the mountains that surrounded Hope Valley that put me at ease.

I hadn't planned on staying as long as I did, but once I got there and remembered how much I loved it, it had been difficult to leave. And meeting Ivy certainly hadn't helped. I kept making excuses to stay, dragging out what was only supposed to have been a couple weeks into several months, and she was the main reason why, whether I wanted to admit it to myself or not.

That first glimpse had been enough to pique my

curiosity. I needed to know the beautiful woman with the pale, creamy complexion and strawberry blonde hair, so I went about doing just that. And the more I got to know, the more she drew me in. It was impossible not to like her.

She had a fiery spirit that intrigued me and turned me on at the same time. She was sweet and hilarious and a little bit crazy. She flitted around like a butterfly hopped up on caffeine. There was never a dull moment when I was with her. As the days turned into weeks, the desire to be near her, to see her smile or watch her laugh, grew into more of a need until that need finally morphed into an obsession.

It was because of that obsession that I ended up pulling the dickiest of dick moves and running out on her. It was why I took off without a goodbye, creeping out of the bed we'd spent hours in before she woke up. Because I knew if I didn't get the hell out of there right then, I'd end up staying. For her. And that was a road I *never* planned on going down again.

I left the ranch determined to get back to my old life and push her from my mind. To live up to the reputation I had on the circuit of being a playboy bachelor, the man who would never settle down, but I couldn't do it. I could play at the charm and the flirting, but I couldn't bring myself to look in another woman's direction. Not without seeing Ivy's face. My goddamn dick wouldn't even react, for fuck's sake.

It didn't matter how beautiful a woman was. If it wasn't for the fact that I beat off at least once a day to the memory of my one and only night with Ivy, I would have freaked the fuck out and run straight to a doctor to find out what was wrong. But I didn't need medical intervention to know the issue.

My traitorous dick wouldn't get hard for anyone but *her*.

The noise in the bar suddenly swelled, and I knew, without having to turn around, what had caused the atmosphere to go wired. But still, I couldn't stop my body from shifting on my stool and my eyes from trailing over my shoulder to see who had just walked in.

My heart started beating faster as my stomach sank like it was suddenly coated in lead when Dusty Silver walked in with an air like he owned the place. That was what his reputation had earned him after all these years. He was the closest thing to royalty we had on the circuit. A renowned bull rider back in his day, he'd taken it all at the World Championship not once but three times over his career. Instead of retiring when the time came, taking all the money he'd made for himself and holing up on a tropical island somewhere, he'd decided to train young bull riders.

He'd been my mentor, teaching me everything I knew

today. But he'd also been much more than that. He'd been like family to me—almost like a second father. At least until I hit a rough patch a while back.

I'd gotten stuck in my own head and it had affected my rides. I'd gone from placing near the top at every rodeo I competed in to barely scraping by. It was a bad look for him. I'd lost my usefulness, so he'd dropped me faster than I could blink and took on another rider. Vance Grimes, his shiny new protégé, was a piece of shit who thought way too highly of himself, and for some reason, he had a grudge against me. I wasn't surprised to see him following behind Dusty like a little puppy dog, happy to lick the old man's boots.

I twisted back around, facing forward before I drew either of their attention. I was in a piss-poor mood as it was, I didn't need to deal with Vance's bullshit or Dusty's judgmental looks.

"Oh my *God*," a breathy, feminine voice said close to my ear, pulling my attention from the last two people I wanted to deal with. "Are you Connor Bennett?"

I groaned internally, doing my best to keep the annoyance I felt off my face as I slowly swiveled my head in the direction of the woman who had squeezed herself between my barstool and the empty one beside it. It shouldn't have been so hard for me to curl my lips into some semblance of a grin, especially given the fact that the woman was a serious looker, but I really wasn't in the mood.

I sent a silent curse of disgust to my dick. The fucking thing was as limp as an overcooked noodle. This time last year, I wouldn't have hesitated to play up the charm, laying it on as thick as necessary in order to get this woman into my bed for a night. *It wouldn't have taken too much*, I thought as I took in her smile. I could tell from the gleam in her eye and the way her red-painted lips curved up in the corners, that was why she'd approached me in the first place. She liked the way I looked, heard of my reputation, and was eager for a ride all her own.

But this wasn't a year ago. Now . . . well, now there wasn't so much as a stirring, not even a little tickle down below the belt. *Goddamn it.*

"That I am, darlin'," I answered, easily slipping into the role I always played while I traveled on the circuit. "I take it you're a fan?"

Her tongue peeked out and dragged across her bottom lip as her lids lowered sensuously. I held my breath and waited for any signs of life from my dick. Still nothing. "Oh yeah. I'm a big fan," she simpered, reaching out to drag the pointed tip of her long nail down my arm. "You know, I came here tonight hoping to run into you."

I was sure she'd come hoping to run into *any* bull rider, not me specifically. I knew her type. Woman was a buckle bunny through and through, not that I judged. I'd sampled my fair share over the years. But odds were, if there had been another guy in this bar who'd placed better than I did, got himself the bigger buckle, she'd have sidled up to him, not me.

"Saw you ride tonight. It really was somethin'. You just look so . . . masculine up there on those bulls." She leaned in closer to try and draw attention to her cleavage. "So *hot*."

Fucking hell, I thought. *I should have just gone straight to my room and gotten drunk there.*

"So, I was thinkin'. Maybe we could get out of here. Go somewhere a little more . . . private." The woman's fingertips danced their way up my arm to my shoulder before she flattened her hand and rubbed it over my chest. I had to hand it to her, she had confidence, that was for goddamn sure. Usually it would have made me rock hard, but I couldn't help but compare her to the woman who was driving me insane. The bane of my existence. "If you know what I mean."

I knew exactly what she meant. Hell, she was being about as subtle as a bull moose during mating season.

But it didn't matter. It was never going to happen. Her blonde hair didn't have the shade of red in it like Ivy's. Her plain blue eyes didn't shine like sapphires the way Ivy's did. Her complexion was too tanned, unlike Ivy's fair, creamy skin I had spent hours running my tongue and lips over until every single inch seared into my brain. Even her smell threw me off, the overly powdery fragrance making the inside of my nose itch like I was fighting off a sneeze. Nothing like Ivy's fresh, sunny lemon and basil scent.

"Appreciate the offer, darlin', but I'm gonna have to pass."

She straightened up, the seductive look melting off of her made-up face. "Your loss, cowboy," she issued before pushing away from the bar and moving on to the next guy.

I was sure she was right.

I tossed back the rest of my whiskey and sent a glare down at my dick. This was all his fault.

"Well, well, well. Look who it is," a voice said from behind me.

Goddamn it.

Just like that, my night got even fucking worse.

Chapter Two

CONNOR

"**Y**ou looked so lonely over here all by yourself. Figured I'd keep you company."

I turned my head slowly, my expression void of any emotion. "Don't feel you need to do me any favors," I deadpanned.

His grin was smug as hell, showcasing unnaturally-perfect white capped teeth. It was taking everything I had not to knock those teeth down his throat.

He hefted himself onto the stool beside me, the stench of the cheap cologne he'd obviously bathed in giving me an immediate headache. The guy was fucking good on a bull, as much as I hated to admit that. Most of the time we were neck and neck. That was the reason Dusty had taken him on, after all. He wouldn't back a nobody. But on top of being an asshole, he also didn't know how to spend the money he'd been coming into lately if the eye-watering stink coming off him and the tacky veneers were anything to go on.

"Seems like a runnin' theme for you lately, huh?" His grin grew even wider. "Or maybe you just keep strikin' out."

Christ, I really hated this guy.

I waved to get the bartender's attention, pointing at my empty glass when I caught his eye. The smart thing to do was leave, but I didn't want to give this prick the satisfaction of thinking he'd run me out. For some reason, he'd created this competition between us, and it extended beyond those eight seconds in the arena.

Dusty wasn't the only person in my life to throw me over for this piece of shit.

I snatched up the fresh whiskey as soon as the bartender placed it in front of me and drank down half before turning to face the guy. "Do I need to be concerned with how much you're watchin' me, Grimes? I gotta tell you, this shit's getting a little creepy."

His cheeks flushed with anger as his expression grew hard. "Amber says hi, by the way."

It was a well-placed shot, bringing her up, and I fucking hated that it still managed to get to me, even after all this time. Fortunately, I managed to keep my expression neutral and my body loose, masking the raging storm inside of me that was coiling around my muscles and heating my blood to a boil at the mention of my ex's name.

Instead of letting him think he'd gotten the best of me, I allowed my lips to curl up in a smile just as cocky as the one he'd been wearing when he'd sauntered up to me. "Is that right? You might want to try stepping up your game if I'm still on your girlfriend's mind like that. You know, there are books that can teach you how to please a woman."

That flush grew even deeper at the realization that he'd set himself up for that one. "She's not just my girlfriend anymore." He adopted that look of arrogance again that made it so hard not to punch him. "She's my fiancée now." It took all my strength to keep from squeezing the glass in my hand so hard the fucking thing shattered. I would have been lying if I said I hadn't seen this coming. On top of being a bitch, Amber was the most conniving, opportunistic woman I'd ever known. I wasn't surprised in the least. But that didn't mean it didn't feel like I'd had a hot poker shoved into my chest.

But I would be damned if I let that show. Instead, I reached over and clapped him on his shoulder just as my cellphone started to ring from where I'd placed it on the bar when I first showed up. "Congratulations, buddy. Should take the sting out of placing below me tonight, huh?" I said with a saccharine grin as I stood from my stool and fished a few bills out of my wallet, tossing them on the bar—more than enough to cover my tab and his. "This round's on me then. Enjoy my sloppy seconds while it lasts."

With that, I snatched up my phone and swiped the screen, brushing that fucker off before he could get another word out. "Hello," I answered as I turned on the heel of my boot and started toward the exit.

"Glad you aren't so famous you don't answer your phone."

Pushing my encounter with that jackass out of my head, I smiled at the sound of Zach's voice, his humor carrying clearly through the line. I started for the exit, making sure not to limp as I moved through the crowd. Last thing I needed was for someone to get a picture of that shit and post it all over social media, or to give Vance the opportunity to start spreading rumors. My agent was still finessing some of my sponsors that had gotten a little shaky after the first injury, assuring them I was good to go. I made really good money rodeoing, but those sponsorships were key. The underwear ad I'd done a few years back still made me a shitload of cash.

"I try to keep a firm hold on my roots. Keeps me humble."

His bark of laughter rang in my ear. "Humble my ass,"

he ribbed. "Now a good time? Sounds kind of rowdy where you are. Need to call me back?"

"No. It's all good. I'm on my way out anyway."

I could hear Zach's smile carrying through the line as he said, "You sure? I'd hate to interrupt whatever game you were probably runnin' on those poor, unsuspecting ladies down there."

I managed a chuckle that I hoped didn't sound as hollow as it felt as I pushed out of the bar and stepped into the dimly lit parking lot. I didn't used to mind my reputation. Hell, after everything with Amber imploded, I did what I could to live up to it since I sure as hell wasn't going down that road ever again. But lately it had started to feel more like a heavy weight around my shoulders, dragging me down, than something fun.

Not that I was going to bother saying any of that to him. There was no way I was getting into the fact that there was no woman tonight, or hadn't been any other night for months. Not since before I left his ranch and headed back out on the circuit. And I sure as hell wasn't getting into *why*. He was friends with both me and Ivy, and I was sure he'd skin my ass alive if he knew I'd touched her.

That was a fight I didn't feel like having.

"Yeah, well, you know me," I said, adopting a noncommittal tone. "Just livin' the dream." I quickly moved to change the subject as I closed in on the motel right across the street from the bar. I could have afforded something nicer like a room at the five-star hotel that douche-nozzle Grimes was staying at ten minutes away, but I wasn't picky about where I slept. As long as it was clean and had a bed, I was good. "How is everything goin' over there. How is I—Rae?"

I had to swallow down the desire to inquire about Ivy and quickly covered it up by asking about his fiancée instead. Zach had always been a bit of a grumpy bastard, but when Rae came into his life, she managed to cast light on the shadows of his past. She chased away my friend's demons—literally and figuratively. I might be against commitment like that for myself now, but I was happy for Zach that he'd found a good one.

"Everything's great. Rae's really kickin' ass managing the ranch. Really whipping this place into shape. And speakin' of kicking ass, we watched your ride tonight. You killed it, brother. Proud of you."

I paused halfway through the parking lot. "You guys watched?"

"Of course we did. We watch all your televised rides if we can. Even had a few friends over. Hal, Raylan, Ivy, and a few others. Kind of made a thing out of it."

My chest started to warm at the knowledge that my friends had been watching my rides . . . at least until I remembered what happened afterward. "Did you watch . . ." I cleared my throat and tried to swallow down the knot that had suddenly formed. "Did you guys watch everything?"

I knew the answer just as soon as Zach started laughing. "You mean the interview afterward? Yeah, man. We all watched that. I bet that chick's the one you plan on hooking up with tonight, huh? Tell me I'm right. I bet Rae twenty bucks it would be her."

Fuck my life.

I let out a heavy sigh and reached up to rub at the pulsing throb that had started in the middle of my forehead as I crossed the quiet asphalt road between the bar's parking lot and the motel's.

It wasn't out of the ordinary for me to give an interview after a ride, especially when I'd placed at the very top. They had to be my least favorite part of this job, but tonight's was made even worse when an overzealous buckle bunny came running up when I wasn't looking and launched herself at me, grabbing hold of my face and sealing her lips on mine right in front of the reporter and camera man. The jostle had sent a sharp stab of pain through my knee, knocking the wind right out of my lungs, and instead of pushing her away, I ended up holding on to the woman to keep from toppling over, playing off the encounter with a laugh and the charm I was known for. Anything to keep from showing how much pain I was in.

As soon as the cameras stopped rolling I did the best I could to disentangle from the woman without causing a scene. My gut twisted painfully as I reached the door to my room and pulled my key from my pocket. "So . . . you *all* saw that then?"

Please say no. Please say no, I silently chanted. Maybe I'd get lucky and Ivy had left early or something.

"Yep," he answered with ease. *Goddamn it!* "So am I right? Did I win that twenty from Rae?"

I heaved out a heavy sigh and let myself into my room, flipping on the light as I entered. The place had been built sometime in the eighties, and while it was clean, it hadn't been updated in some time. The bedding looked like something you'd find at your grandmother's house. A floral monstrosity that matched perfectly with the doilies covering the ugly yellow pine furniture.

As soon as I shut the door behind me, I let go of all pretenses that I was fine and hobbled over to the bed, plopping down on the edge and straightening out my leg so I could rub at the pain in my knee. "Sorry, man. Looks like you lose this time."

"Damn it. She's never gonna let me live this down."

I faked another laugh while my insides churned like the ocean in the middle of a hurricane. I hated that Ivy had seen that. It was just another thing to add to the list of reasons why I was the world's biggest asshole. There were a million better ways I could have handled things after our night together, but I'd freaked out. She'd made me feel things I swore to myself I was never going to feel again. As I moved inside her, looking down at her writhing body beneath mine, there had been a moment—a flash, there and gone in the blink of an eye—where I could have sworn I'd seen my forever shimmering in her sapphire eyes, and I lost it.

I was sure Ivy already hated me for how I'd bailed on her, and I couldn't fault her one damn bit. But if she didn't, seeing that chick clinging to me like a spider monkey during that interview would most definitely be the final nail in the coffin. Not that it mattered. That one night was all we were ever going to have. I left for a reason. I couldn't give that woman what she deserved. She was too damn good for me in every single way, and I didn't have a doubt in my mind that she knew that now.

We were better off like this. *She* was better off. And hopefully, if I repeated that in my head enough, I would finally start to believe it. Maybe then I would quit thinking about her. I would stop drafting and deleting text messages to her every damn day.

"Well, I guess I should let you go. Let you get back to your night. I'm sure you have better things to do than talk to me," Zach said after we shot the shit for a few more minutes, catching each other up on our lives. Sad thing was, talking to him was the most enjoyment I'd had in way too damn long. It made me miss Hope Valley and Safe Haven Ranch. Made me miss the months I'd spent there.

It made me miss *her*.

I preferred talking to him than the silence of my motel room, but instead of saying as much, I made sure my tone was light and casual as I said, "Yeah, for sure. But I'll be seein' you in just a few weeks. Can't get married without your best man, right?"

The smile in his voice was clear as a bell. "Christ, I can't believe the wedding's almost here."

"You get cold feet, I've got you covered," I teased.

He let out a short chuckle. "Not a chance in hell. I feel like I've been waiting my whole life to make that woman mine. I would have married her a million times by now if she hadn't insisted on goin' all out. I can't fuckin' wait."

"I'm really happy for you, brother," I said, a genuine smile pulling at the corners of my mouth. "Really happy. Rae's great. And there's no one better equipped to deal with your grumpy ass."

"Don't I know it," he said jovially. "Well, I'll let you go.

See you soon, man. In the meantime, keep kickin' ass out there."

"Will do."

I hung up and dropped the phone onto the bed, falling backward onto the mattress as the silence surrounded me. There were only a few weeks until I'd see Ivy again, and something told me I needed every minute of the time between now and then to prepare to face her.

Chapter Three

IVY

My mother always warned me never to get involved with a bull rider.

Okay, not really. But she should have. It was sound advice.

Of course, she'd never known any bull riders, but if she had she most certainly would have warned me against getting involved with one. *Especially* if that bull rider was Connor *freaking* Bennett. Not that her warnings would have mattered much. After all, I'd always had a bit of a taste for trouble.

In the back of my mind I'd known a man who had as much charm and swagger as Connor did would end up being nothing but trouble. I smelled it on him the very first time we met, but instead of seeing him for what he was—a walking, talking red flag with a great, dimpled smile and an even better ass—I played right into his hand. In my defense, he really had pulled out all the stops to win me over.

My cellphone chimed with a text, pulling me out of my head and the memory from a few nights ago when I saw that woman launch herself at him on camera and try to fish his tonsils out with her tongue. And that son of a bitch just lapped it up.

I let out a frustrated groan at having gotten lost in thoughts of that asshole *again.* It seemed like no matter how many mornings I woke up and told myself I was not going to think about Connor Bennett, he would somehow manage to niggle his way into my mind whenever I wasn't paying attention. The littlest thing would spark a memory, and I'd fall right back down that rabbit hole without even realizing.

I did my best to push the latest thoughts of Connor Bennett to the back of my mind, shoving them down into the deepest, darkest cobwebbed corner, and focused on the breathing exercises I learned from the meditation app my friend Holly talked me into downloading a couple weeks back. So far I wasn't very good at it. Meditating required clearing the mind and being still in the present for an extended period of time, something I had never been good at.

I could handle yoga, thanks to the lessons my mom's

great aunt Silvia had started giving me back when I was still a toddler, but that was only because by the time I started getting bored in one position, we were moving on to the next one. I was an active kid. I spent most of my early years covered in dirt and mud from hours and hours spent outside. I always managed to get into something, and not much had changed since growing up.

I liked to stay busy. I tended to get bored easily, and when that happened, it usually resulted in me getting into some kind of trouble.

I was the child whose parents were always getting calls from the school because I couldn't keep my mouth shut during class. Bedtime was a nightmare for my poor mom. Unless she managed to run me ragged in the evenings, I was a little terror who would climb out of bed a million times for a million different reasons before finally passing out a good three hours *after* I was supposed to be asleep.

On top of being busy, I had also been a little wild. Although most of what I got up to was relatively harmless, I had driven my mom and stepdad up the wall, seeing as more than once I had been escorted home by the cops after one of my many stunts.

There was that time when I was sixteen and got caught skinny dipping in the creek that ran along old Tolliver Mill Road. A couple years later, after binging all the *Fast and Furious* movies, I convinced myself I would be a natural at drag racing and challenged a couple of the guys on the football team to a race. My mom had screamed at me for at least an hour about the dangers I had put myself in, but once she stormed off after burning herself out, her husband, Micah, asked if I at least won, high-fiving me when I told him I'd smoked those losers.

Then I went through a minor anarchist phase where I convinced the entire senior class to stage a walkout in protest of the dress code the district was trying to enforce that would strip everyone of their individuality and was created to make the girls feel like it was our fault if boys popped a boner and could no longer concentrate because, Lord forbid, we wore shorts or a skirt that didn't come all the way down to our knees.

I'd gotten more than my fair share of speeding and parking tickets—I was shit at parallel parking—and was busted once or twice for underage drinking. Then there was that one time a few of my friends and I tried to sneak backstage during a Civil Corruption concert and had to be carried out—literally—by burly security guards. We didn't talk about that particular incident, mainly because it made the tabloids. While I found it hilarious—I even framed the picture they ran with the article of me being carted out over some dude's shoulder in a fireman's hold—my folks did *not*.

My mom claimed she had to start coloring her hair

years ago because I'd driven her so crazy she'd gone gray early. My stepdad was a cop with the local police department, and thanks to my shenanigans, Micah had to deal with his fair share of shit from his partner and other co-workers. Apparently, they had started placing bets on when I'd get into trouble next.

I did my best to tame a bit of that wildness as I got older, but that was easier said than done. It was like trying to breathe when there was no air or trying to stop your heart from beating. It was that side of me that was so drawn to Connor in the first place, even though I knew he was all kinds of trouble.

I tried ignoring him at first, but the man made it way too damn hard. He was always *there*. He went out of his way to win me over, and I got swept up in him, falling for all the pretty words and actions. What woman wouldn't fall for a man who brought her wildflowers he picked himself every day or showed up at her job to sweep her off for a picnic lunch he packed himself? We had inside jokes and shared about our lives. He'd even confessed that he feared the day when he could no longer do what he loved, and what that would mean. How he tied so much of who he was into being a bull rider that he wasn't sure how to exist outside of it. When he told me he'd never shared those concerns with anyone else, I'd felt honored.

He made me feel like I was important to him, like I was special. Then he made me feel like the world's biggest fool.

I spent months holding on to my anger with an iron grip so I would never forget. If I didn't forget I wouldn't fall for that bullshit the next time. Not that there would ever *be* a next time. As far as Connor Bennet went, I'd learned my lesson and I would not be making the same mistake twice.

I had hoped to never see that asshole's charming, chiseled, stupidly perfect face ever again. Unfortunately, the bastard was tight with Zach Paulson, the son of the family I worked for and the soon-to-be husband of one of my closest friends. Escaping him completely wasn't an option, unless I wanted to quit my job and ghost Rae, two things I would never do. I adored Rae, the former big city celebutant-turned-rancher's-fiancée. She was one of my favorite people, and had taken to the slower pace of ranching life like she was born for it. She'd traded in her stilettos for boots and her designer dresses for jeans. If you looked at her now, you would never guess she'd once been a part of the LA party scene.

As for my career, working as the hospitality manager for Second Hope Lodge, the rustic yet swanky resort-style hotel that was a part of Safe Haven Ranch, was my dream job. I wasn't going to let anyone run me out.

Normally, Connor only popped up once in a blue

moon whenever a rodeo brought him out this way. He was usually too busy getting his ass thrown off the backs of angry bulls and screwing his way through every buckle bunny on the circuit to make regular trips, but with Zach and Rae's wedding just around the corner, I was going to be forced to see him sooner than I'd hoped.

I had been trying my best to prepare myself for the inevitable. My plan was to fake it, to smile and laugh and act like I didn't hate the very ground that asshole walked on. After all, what was a few days of pretending if it meant making sure my friends had the wedding of their dreams?

I could totally do it. And if not, my Plan B was to act like I didn't recognize him.

There was also the tiny fact that I didn't want him to know I was still angry and hurt that I woke up to find the man I slept with only hours earlier had taken off in the middle of the night. That kind of burn stayed with a person, singeing their ego until there was little left. It wasn't just the sting of his rejection, but also the humiliation that came with *how* he left. The man made me believe there was something big happening between us, then he bounced, leaving behind nothing more than a one-word note that he'd scribbled on the back of a crumpled receipt he had probably found stuffed in his pocket.

Thanks.

That was it.

That was all he'd said.

He'd worked for *months* to get into my pants, practically the entire time he was on the ranch, supposedly resting his injured knee, and when I finally let him take me to bed, thinking all the shit he'd spewed had been genuine, that was all he'd left me with. *Thanks*. Talk about a slap in the face.

There hadn't been a single phone call or text. I would have accepted a smoke signal or homing pigeon, for Christ's sake. But there was nothing. I had been well and truly ghosted.

The thing was, I didn't start out with any expectations. If he'd told me from the beginning that it was just sex, I would have been fine with that. It wasn't like I had visions of white picket fences and two point five kids dancing in my head, and the man was the living example of sex in a pair of cowboy boots and faded jeans. When he pulled off that baseball cap he favored and twisted it backward, my stomach never failed to erupt with butterflies. But he pulled out all the stops to make me believe it was so much more than that. The things he said, the things he did . . .

He made me feel like I was the only woman that existed for him. He not only accepted that wild streak of mine, but he seemed to actually enjoy it—doing what he could to coax it out of me. I'd never felt so wanted, so craved and desired, in all my life, not to mention the sex.

God, the sex.

I wish I could say it was bad, or even just average. I would have gladly settled for the kind of bang that was good enough to get the job done in the moment but eventually faded from a person's mind. Unfortunately, I hadn't been that lucky. That son of a bitch *seriously* knew what he was doing. Not that I should have been surprised, given his track record. Apparently Connor had a reputation throughout the rodeo circuit. He'd been dubbed the playboy bull-riding bachelor. But I let myself forget about the stories I'd heard and the things I'd seen on the internet.

I'd convinced myself that the cockiness and charisma were a part he played for the cameras, that the real man behind the swagger and charm was so much deeper and softer and more caring. I felt like I had been given the gift of seeing the *real* him.

I was wrong.

But none of that mattered anymore. What I *thought* we had was over. If he hadn't made that perfectly clear with his scribbled *thanks*, that lip-lock on camera the other night certainly did it. I was back to living my own life, reminding myself every few hours when he popped into my head against my will, I wasn't supposed to be thinking about him any longer.

Grabbing my phone from where it rested on my desk, I

swiped the screen to read the message that had just come through.

Rae: *Don't forget about tonight. Ladies' night at the Tap Room. And no excuses that you're too busy!*

I let out a low chuckle and shook my head, quickly typing out a response that I hadn't forgotten and I'd be there.

After all, ladies' night was just what I needed to get my mind off the man who didn't deserve a second thought.

Chapter Four

IVY

I finished typing my last email of the day and sent it off before rocking back in my chair and pulling in a centering breath. Twisting toward the window to my left, I took in the beautiful view beyond the glass as twilight spread like a blanket over the valley. My office sat on the second floor of Second Hope Lodge, giving me an unobstructed view of the ranch stretching out below and the mountains beyond surrounding my small town. If I thought that it was beautiful just then, it was even better in the winter when everything was covered in fresh white snow, making it look and feel like the whole town was in a snow globe.

I was four years old when my mom moved us to Hope Valley, but the beauty of this place still managed to take my breath away all these years later. I might not have been born in Hope Valley, but it was home, and would be forever. I couldn't imagine wanting to live anywhere else.

Standing, I placed my hands on the small of my back and arched my spine, giving it a much-needed stretch. I shut everything down and grabbed my purse, flipping the light switch off as I exited my office and headed down the hall to the main staircase that would take me out into the great room.

The massive space was the main hub of the lodge. Everything about it screamed cozy country living, from the high wood-beamed ceilings to the stone fireplace that was big enough to warm the entire area in the winter. The room was decked out in buttery-soft leather couches the color of cognac, and the rich wood-paneled walls were covered in paintings or sepia-tinted photographs of vast fields of flowers or horses and cows. Those that didn't contain art were lined with custom-built shelves full of books that spanned across any genre a person could want.

It wasn't uncommon to find guests dotted around, either cozied up on the couches reading from our vast selection, enjoying a coffee from the restaurant off the back of the great room or a cocktail from our bar, Saddled and Spurred, off to the left.

The reception desk, where guests checked in, stood between the branched-off grand staircase. Tucked into a nook beneath the left staircase was the activities desk where I spent at least half of my workday, signing guests up for all the different excursions we offered on the ranch.

It would have been faster to go out the employee exit where my car was parked, but I liked to end each day here, taking time to feel things out and keep my finger on the pulse of the place. And more times than not, I'd run into a guest who had a question I was more than happy to answer.

"You finally heading out?" Becky asked as my heels clicked against the scraped wood floors at the bottom of the steps.

I turned to face the reception desk with a big smile. Becky Hightower might have been up there in years, but the woman didn't know the meaning of the word slow. She and her husband, Bill, had retired a million times, first from the Tap Room, their family's bar. Then from this very ranch, handing it down to their grandson Zach. But none of those times ever seemed to stick for long. Hell, they were the brains behind opening Second Hope Lodge and played active roles in its day-to-day operations. Becky herself managed the place and had been the one to interview me before hiring me a few years ago.

"Yep. Just have to run home real quick to change before I meet up with Rae and the rest of the girls."

Her grin deepened the smile lines around her mouth and eyes that had formed thanks to the long, happy life she had lived so far. "Good. I'm glad you're getting out. You need to live, Ivy girl. You work too damn much."

She wasn't exactly wrong. Most days I didn't leave here until the sun had already gone down, but you know what they said about doing what you love. "I like my job," I said with an easy shrug. "I love it here."

"And we love having you, sweetheart, but your work can't be everything. You're still young. You should be out living it up, having fun. Meeting fine young men," she said with a waggle of her brows.

I tossed my hair over my shoulders on a laugh. "Don't let my parents hear you say that. According to them I've had more than my fair share of fun. If it wasn't for the fact this is a small town, I'd have the arrest record to prove it."

"Okay, fine. Maybe don't go buck wild, but this town is full of fine men who would give their left arm for a shot with you. You should be out there leaving a trail of broken hearts in your wake."

Oh, if only it were that easy. What I didn't bother saying was that I *wished* I could put myself out there and start dating again. I'd always enjoyed it. Unfortunately, ever since Connor, it seemed a switch had been flipped and I couldn't bring myself to accept any of the offers that had come my way these past few months. It was like that asshole had managed to break something inside of me, making it impossible for me to say yes to another man.

It was reason enough to punch him right in his perfectly proportioned face.

"Who knows, maybe tonight I'll get lucky," I offered, even though I knew I'd most likely end up going home alone like I had every single night for the past few months. That knowledge set me on edge, because after witnessing that kiss, it was obvious Connor wasn't having the same issue.

"Fingers crossed, darlin'. Either way, enjoy yourself tonight, and I'll see you tomorrow."

"See you," I said as I spun on the sharp point of my heel and proceeded to slam into a wall of firm, hot muscle. "Oh my God."

"Whoa," a deep, husky voice said as I dragged my eyes up the broad chest covered by a soft navy T-shirt. "You okay?"

"I'm so sorry. I wasn't watching where I was going," I insisted as I finally met the gaze of the man I'd collided with.

"It was an accident. You have nothing to apologize for."

"Mr. Fine," I greeted as a slight warmth filled my cheeks.

It was ironic that Becky and I were just talking about attractive men only moments before, because the guy standing in front of me certainly lived up to his last name, that was for damn sure. Tanner Fine had been at the lodge for three days, and everyone was losing their minds. The women couldn't get over how attractive he was and the men were drooling over the professional athlete in their midst. Apparently the guy was a famous hockey player for a team in DC. He sure was built well enough to be one. I couldn't imagine what it would feel like to have the guy crash into you on the ice. He was the human equivalent of a brick wall. To say having him here had made things interesting would have been an understatement. He was all anyone had been able to talk about for days. I had to admit, even I wasn't immune to all that he was. I'd been more than a little flustered during our brief encounters so far.

"Please, call me Tanner. And you're Ivy, right?"

I nodded, the warmth in my cheeks intensifying beneath his gaze. In the past I wouldn't have hesitated to shoot my shot with a guy like Tanner, but that was before stupid *freaking* Connor. Still, I couldn't help my body's reaction to having the attention of such an attractive man. "That's right. How has your stay with us been so far? Are you enjoying yourself?"

He grinned at me, and I waited to feel the flutter of butterflies in my belly, but it never came. It was a good smile. A *great* smile, actually. But it didn't have dimples. It didn't have that tiny hint of wickedness that promised something wild and crazy and reckless.

"I am, thanks," he said, his charm more All-American than the playboy type I found myself most drawn to lately. *Damn it.* "Did some fly fishing today. It was exactly what I needed. Quiet and relaxing."

"Good, I'm glad. You know, if quiet is what you're after, there are some incredible hiking trails all around here. I'd be more than happy to sign you up with one of our guides."

Tanner tucked his hands into his pockets, his smile going crooked in the most adorable way, showcasing a bright white smile. "I don't suppose I could get you to be my guide for one of those hikes?"

The sound of Becky clearing her throat from behind me was obnoxiously loud. I cast a quick glance over my shoulder, throwing a glare her way that said *pipe down, woman* before looking back at the big wall of beefcake. "Sorry, that's not really my area of expertise. Trust me, you don't want me as your guide."

He took a step closer, lowering his voice. "Then maybe you'd just like to go with me," he suggested, and I silently cursed Connor for ruining *everything*.

"I really appreciate the offer, but things are kind of crazy right now," I said gently, hating turning down a man who, at least on paper, seemed like an absolute catch. It pissed me off that I couldn't get my head on straight, even months later. I really needed to get my shit together.

He started walking backward slowly. "I understand. Maybe some other time. You know . . . when things are a little less crazy."

"Yeah, maybe."

I really hoped that happened sooner rather than later.

THE TAP ROOM WAS ALREADY BUSY BY THE TIME I arrived there later that evening. I pushed through the door and stepped inside, scanning all the familiar faces in search of my crew. That was one of the things I liked most about living in a small town, you knew most everybody. It could be a pain, especially when you were prone to trouble and trying to hide it from your parents, and the gossip mill worked faster in smaller towns, but mostly, I loved knowing everyone around me. It was a tight-knit community, and I loved being a part of it.

Something caught my attention from the corner of my eye and I turned to see Rae standing at a round high-top table equal distance between the bar and dance floor. Our other friends, Lennix, Holly, and Holly's sister Sunny, were already there with drinks as well. Aside from Rae, the rest of us had practically grown up together.

I moved through the crowd, offering smiles and waves and returning hellos to the people I passed along the way.

"You made it," Rae said happily, pulling me in for a quick hug. "Here, I ordered for you already."

She slid the blond ale I favored my way and I quickly picked up the glass, taking a much-needed sip. "Appreciate it. I told you I was coming."

"I know, but you'd usually still be at the lodge right about now," Lennix added, arching a brow in a silent dare for me to tell her she was wrong.

I narrowed my eyes at her. "You know, you and your grandmother are too damn much alike."

She smiled proudly. "My mom and dad tell me that same thing all the time." Of course she would take pride in the fact that she drove her parents to the brink of insanity. That was a shared quality that she and I had bonded over in the past, but she wasn't supposed to use it against me.

"Well, excuse me for liking my job. I figured you of all people would understand. It's supposed to be your night off and you came out with your friends to *your own bar*."

She laughed, lifting her beer to her lips and drinking. "All right, point taken. I'll cut you some slack."

"Speaking of your job . . ." Lennix wiggled her brows. "I heard a particularly hot guest asked you out today."

Damn it, Becky!

"It was nothing," I insisted.

Lennix shot me a look that said she knew I was full of shit. "Didn't seem like nothing to grandma. She said he seemed really into you."

Rae bounced in her seat. "Ooh, was it that guest at the lodge everyone at the ranch is talking about? I only got a brief glimpse of him once, but he was *gorgeous*." She pointed a finger at each of us. "And if any of you tell Zach I said that I'll lie through my teeth."

"Isn't he some kind of athlete?" Holly asked.

"He plays hockey," I answered before I could stop myself. "And yes, he's hot, and he asked me out, but it would be totally inappropriate to get involved with a guest."

Sunny reared back on her chair. "Says who? Is that a rule or something?"

I took a big gulp of my beer. "Well, no. Not technically. But what the hell would I do with a famous hockey player?" I scoffed.

"Oh, I can think of quite a few things," Sunny said, garnering a laugh from everyone else.

I balled up a napkin and threw it at her. "It doesn't matter. I already turned him down."

I hadn't been able to bring myself to tell my friends about what had happened with Connor. The whole situation was too embarrassing, and I didn't want to rehash my own stupidity, but I wondered if they'd push so hard for me to date if they knew.

"Then take it back," Rae insisted, like it made all the sense in the world. "The man didn't lose interest just because you shot him down once."

Holly nodded in agreement. "She's right. Find him and tell him you changed your mind."

Rae pulled in a sharp gasp and slapped a palm down on the table, her eyes going wide with excitement. "You know what you should do? You should invite him to the wedding next week."

I choked on the sip of beer I'd just taken. "I'm not asking some guy I don't know to be my date to your wedding."

She lifted her hands in curiosity. "Why not? I mean, it's basically just one big-ass party. Think about it. An open bar, great music, dancing, and if he turns out to be a dud, you'll be surrounded by your friends to keep you company."

She had a point. There was also the silver lining that I wouldn't be alone the first time I was forced to see Connor again.

Chapter Five

CONNOR

The moment I guided my truck through the gate and beneath the sign that read Safe Haven Ranch, it felt like a valve in my chest had opened, releasing all this pressure I didn't realize had been building up. That was the effect this place had on me. The town, the ranch, all of it.

Being back here was a balm to my soul. I had a week here to celebrate my best friend's wedding and to soak up all the peace and comfort this place had to offer before heading back out on the road. I could have used a longer break. My body was feeling the effects of my age and my profession, but I didn't know what the hell to do with myself if I wasn't riding. I usually liked to stick around and help Zach run the ranch, but he'd be taking off with Rae for their honeymoon right after the big day.

I hit the button on the door panel to lower the windows and inhaled deeply, pulling all the familiar scents into my lungs. The earthy smells of hay, grass, and wildflowers baking in the warmth of the sun. The smell of the animals out in the pasture. All of it was more comforting than a security blanket or a home-cooked meal from your momma.

I turned the radio's volume down so I could hear the crunch of my tires on the gravel. I came to the split in the road that would either take me toward the main ranch house where Zach and Rae lived and the big barn beyond, or to Second Hope Lodge. I made the left toward the lodge where Zach said he'd be waiting.

The lodge came into view a few minutes later. Where a chain hotel would have looked totally out of place, the four-story cabin style structure had been built to belong, just like all the other houses and cabins and out buildings that had been built over the generations. Made of wood and stone with huge panes of glass, it blended seamlessly with the tree-covered foothills it butted against and the mountains beyond that jutted up toward the sky. Whoever had designed the place had done a brilliant job.

As I got closer, my heart began to beat faster, knocking against my ribs. I'd thought about a million times over the past few days what I would say to Ivy when I finally saw her again, but as my truck closed the distance between us, the speech I had prepared, the one I'd spent hours memo-rizing and perfecting, had grown fuzzy as the reality of seeing her went from being a distant thought to a very real thing.

I pulled into the guest lot and threw my truck into park. Most of my visits here were spur of the moment between events, and, more times than not, I'd have to bunk in one of the empty cabins designated for the cowboys who worked for Zach because the lodge was usually fully booked. However, this time around, Zach and Rae had made sure to block off rooms for out-of-town guests coming in for the wedding.

My boots hit the dusty ground, and I stretched my arms upward to work my muscles loose from hours on the road before moving to the bed of the truck and hauling my duffle bag from the back.

With the straps looped over my shoulder, I started toward the massive cabin and took in everything around me. There were people lounging comfortably on the cushy outdoor couches and Adirondack chairs that circled the large stone firepit off to my left. It wouldn't be lit until after the sun went down, but they seemed to be content simply to relax.

There was a group gathered near the edge of the deck, circled around Raylan Bradbury, the lodge's guide for things like fishing, hiking, and trail rides. They all watched with rapt fascination as he spoke animatedly. I'd gone on a couple hikes led by this man who had become a friend over the years, and I wasn't the least bit surprised he had their attention. He was damn good at his job and made every trek he was in charge of enjoyable.

My booted foot hit the bottom step leading up to the wraparound porch just as the front doors of the lodge flew open and two kids burst out on peals of laughter and excitement.

"Whoa," I said on a low chuckle, lifting my arms and taking a quick side-step to avoid collision.

"Whoops!" the little boy, who looked about seven, exclaimed when he almost plowed into me. "Sorry, mister!" he exclaimed over his shoulder without breaking stride as he and the little girl with him continued running down the front steps.

A harried woman followed closely after them. "Henry! Cassie! Slow down! You're going to break your necks or someone else's!"

"Sorry, Mom," the two kids shouted back at the same time.

There was no missing the twitch in the woman's eyelid as she looked up at me apologetically. "Sorry about them."

"No sweat," I offered genuinely.

She glanced back over her shoulder at the man I only just noticed trailing behind her, nearly running into the doorframe as he kept his head twisted back to look at something behind him. "Damn it, Carl. Will you please help me out? Those demon-spawns are just as much yours as they are mine."

I had to curl my lips between my teeth to keep from laughing.

"Yeah, sorry. I just . . ." The man looked slightly shell-shocked as he shook his head and followed after his wife. "Did you see that guy? I could have sworn that was—" Their voices trailed off before I could hear who he thought he saw then cut off completely when I stepped into the lodge, the door closing behind me. I moved deeper into the great room right off the entrance. The beauty of this place never failed to take my breath away. I'd barely had enough time to take it all in when I heard a familiar voice call my name.

My mouth stretched into a smile as I turned and spotted Zach heading in my direction. The man looked the happiest I'd ever seen him in all the years of knowing him. Zach was a great guy, one of the best I'd ever known, but he could be a grumpy bastard at times. He'd always been a bit too serious, but the beaming smile he was wearing transformed him completely. If I hadn't known Rae was perfect for him before, seeing him then would have confirmed it.

"Welcome back," he greeted as he got closer, pulling

me in for a quick, back-slapping hug I gladly returned before dropping my arms and taking a step back.

"Happy to be back." More than he could probably imagine. "Though, I nearly got mowed over by a couple rowdy kids whose mom looked like she could really use a stiff drink."

He let loose a chuckle. "Well, I'm glad you survived. It would suck having to get married without a best man."

"Tell me about it. I almost feel bad for the lady, and her husband was acting like he'd seen a—holy Christ." My jaw nearly fell to the floor. "Is that Tanner Fine?"

Zach glanced over his shoulder at the man I'd just spotted coming out of lodge's restaurant, a to-go cup of coffee in his hand.

As if sensing our attention on him, the man in question turned his head and glanced over at us. He offered a friendly wave and grinned before heading in our direction. "Oh, shit. Tanner Fine is coming over here."

A bark of laughter barreled out of my friend. "Jesus, man. You sound like a fangirl."

"Shh!" I hissed as the two-time Stanley Cup winner and goalie for the Washington Rebels started toward us. The guy was a fucking legend. "Be cool, man."

"Fuckin' hell," my friend muttered under his breath with a shake of his head just as the hockey legend stopped in front of us.

"Hey, man," he greeted Zach, the two of them quickly shaking hands.

"Hey. How was that trail ride yesterday?"

"It was great," the giant of a man offered. "Though I'm sore in places today I've never been sore before."

"Yeah, sittin' on a horse is an experience if you've never done it before, that's for sure." Zach cleared his throat and shot me a quick, knowing smirk. "This is my buddy Conner."

He gave me a small chin tilt. "Nice to meet you. I'm—"

"Tanner Fine," I answered for him, like the guy didn't know his own damn name. I thrust my hand in his direction, acting exactly like the fangirl Zach had accused me of being. "I'm a huge fan. *Huge*."

"Christ's sake," Zach mumbled under his breath. Okay, so maybe I was the one who needed to play it cool. But this was actually all his fault if you thought about it. I mean, how could he not tell me Tanner Fine was staying at his lodge? I knew people with more money than sense liked to come to places like this for a taste of a different kind of life, but as far as I knew, this was the first celebrity guest of Second Hope Lodge.

Not counting Rae's dad, of course. Roan Blackwell was a famous musician, but seeing as he and Rae's mother, Alma, were technically from here, even though it wasn't their permanent residence anymore, they were still considered locals.

He chuckled good-naturedly. "Thanks. Always happy to meet a fan."

"Sorry. I wasn't expecting to run into a hockey legend when I showed up." I cast a quick accusatory glance at my so-called best friend. "What brings you down this way?"

"Just needed a bit of a reset after the season ended," he answered. "Was looking for a bit of quiet and a place where I could recharge my batteries."

"Then you picked the right place," I assured him while clapping Zach on the shoulder. I had to give credit where credit was due. He and his family had built something truly spectacular.

"Yeah, I'm quickly discovering that." His focus shifted to something or someone else halfway through that statement, and a whole different kind of smile pulled at his cheeks.

I twisted my head to see what caught his attention, and just like that, all the air escaped my lungs as though they'd been wrung out like a damp washcloth. Despite knowing this moment was coming, I hadn't been fully prepared to face Ivy. I was hoping for at least a few more hours to get my head screwed on straight so I could talk to her without making a fool of myself.

But it looked like that wasn't going to happen.

The woman in question was currently walking down the grand staircase off the reception area. No, that wasn't right. She wasn't just walking—she was *gliding*. That was the only way to describe it. She looked like some sort of ethereal being floating gracefully down the stairs.

All her silky rose-gold hair was twisted up into a messy bun on the top of her head and secured in place with what looked like a pencil. She was dressed in a white blouse with a frilly collar that was tucked into a simple black pencil skirt that nipped in at her waist and hugged the lush curve of her hips. I didn't need her to turn around to know her ass looked impeccable.

Black framed glasses sat perched on her delicate nose, and her rosy bee-stung lips were puckered into a gentle purse as she stared at the iPad in her hands, studying what-ever was on the screen. I didn't need to see her round eyes to know they were the most breathtaking shade of deep sapphire blue. I'd gotten lost while staring into those big blue doe eyes more times than I could count.

The sounds of the busy lodge muffled around me as my focus narrowed on her. My pulse began to race. I felt the adrenaline course through my veins. It was taking everything to keep my feet rooted to the floor when all they wanted to do was charge in her direction. Even my hands were clenched into tight fists as the urge to reach out and touch her became this visceral thing refusing to be ignored.

"Gentlemen," I vaguely heard Tanner Fine say through the blood rushing in my ears, "if you'll excuse me."

I barely registered what was happening as the huge, hulking guy moved faster than a guy his size should, closing in on the staircase as Ivy's black heels clicked at the base of them.

"What the hell?" I mumbled to myself as Tanner stopped in front of Ivy. She jerked her attention from the iPad with a start, the surprise quickly melting away to recognition a second before her lips curved up into a bright, happy smile.

I stood frozen in place as the guy I *used* to be a fan of reached out and tucked a loose lock of Ivy's hair behind her ear. "What the hell?" I repeated, my voice growing louder.

"Oh, yeah. That," Zach said, his voice full of humor. "That guy's been here about a week now, and he's been crushin' on our girl the whole damn time."

I suddenly understood what people meant when they said to never meet your heroes. It was a shame that Tanner was such a talented hockey player. It was going to make committing murder that much harder to get away with.

IVY

I'd been so focused on the calendar app on my tablet that I didn't realize someone was standing in front of me until a huge, looming shadow blinked out the overhead lights.

"Oh!" I startled at Tanner's sudden appearance right in front of me before blowing at the pieces of hair that had fallen out of my makeshift bun. A smile pulled at my lips. "Hi. Sorry, I didn't see you there." Though I didn't know how that was possible given how massive the man was.

"No problem." He gave me that smile he'd been giving me all week long. The one I was sure melted panties all over the country. "Didn't mean to sneak up on you like that."

"You move really quiet for a guy so . . . big." I choked at my own spit as soon as I realized how that sounded. "I didn't mean—not like *that*. I just meant . . . you're a really big guy, and you're light on your feet." I quickly clamped my mouth shut before I could say anything else to humiliate myself.

He laughed, shaking his head good-naturedly. "I got what you meant. Guess you could say light feet is a part of the job."

I blew at the hair that kept falling across my forehead again before I returned his smile easily. I really appreciated that he went out of his way to make me comfortable after the embarrassing bout of word vomit I'd just suffered. The pads of his large fingers skated across my skin when he reached up to tuck those offending strands of hair behind my ear. I stood still, barely pulling in a breath while I sent up a silent prayer for tingles or butterflies or a rush of blood down south. But all I felt for the gorgeous hunk of man standing before me was kinship.

I had to admit, I'd been giving my friends' suggestion of asking Tanner to Rae's wedding a lot of thought. I felt like I'd gotten to know him a little over the past week he'd been staying with us, and the nice guy vibe I got from him had been consistent. There might not be any chance of romance, but I bet it could be a fun night. But something was holding me back from actually saying the words.

"Oh . . . thanks," I said, my body still reacting with a heated flush to my cheeks despite there being no romantic interest. He was still a gorgeous man, even without the tingles.

"Any time. You know, I was wondering if you'd changed your mind on that hike." He held his hands up innocently. "Just as friends. I promise. I don't know what the rest of your day looks like, but it's really beautiful outside, and I was just thinking that—"

"Ivy."

The blood in my veins crystalized, turning into ice at the sound of his voice. I broke eye contact with Tanner on a slow blink as I silently willed myself to remain calm and collected. This was it—the moment I had been dreading, and although my heart felt like it was about to beat right out of my chest, there was no way I was going to let him see that. Inhaling deeply, I forced myself to face the man I would have gladly ignored for the rest of my life. The moment my gaze landed on his deep umber eyes, a riot of butterflies sparked to life in my belly.

Son of a bitch.

My nightly wish that the man would age poorly during his time away had been for nothing, because, if anything, he looked better than ever. Even in jeans, a faded concert tee, and dusty, well-worn boots, he was most women's wet dream come to life. And that *freaking* backward ballcap he was currently sporting only ramped the asshole's hotness up to eleven.

I couldn't let him see he still had any effect on me, so I forced my mouth to tilt up into a small grin. It was all I could muster, but it was something, at least. "Connor. Hi. It's good to see you."

His chin jerked back, his eyes widening with shock. "It-it is?"

The bewilderment carved into the angular planes of his face and his voice infused me with a sense of strength. The ball was in my court. I could do this, I assured myself. "Yeah. I know Zach's always happy to have you back, and with you being here, it means our friends are that much closer to their big day."

"Yeah. Sure." He nodded slowly as his thick, dark brows lowered over his eyes. It felt like his scrutinizing gaze was trying to drill inside my head to see what I was really thinking, but I held firm, keeping an iron grip on my composure.

Suddenly remembering that there was another person standing in our little huddle, I took the opportunity to make introductions, hoping to shift Connor's focus away from me and onto someone else. "I'm sorry. Connor, have you met Tanner Fine? He's staying with us for a couple weeks."

I didn't miss the way his eyelids narrowed as he took the other man in, his gaze sweeping over him from head to foot and back again, almost like he was trying to size the guy up. Connor was no slouch, that was for damn sure. Bull riding apparently built some serious muscle. Still, Tanner had a couple inches and several pounds of muscle on him. Something told me a fight between these two would not be evenly matched.

"We've met," Connor replied, his voice dull and his jaw ticking. It almost looked like he was jealous of the fact that I was talking to another man, but that was ridiculous.

Wasn't it?

I shook that thought off. It would only lead to more trouble. "Great." That chirped word came out overly enthusiastic, warning me that I was quickly reaching the limit on how much time I could be in Connor's presence. I needed to end this uncomfortable little stand-off and get the hell out of here.

"Well, it was good catching up," I told him, proud that the lie at least sounded believable. "But it's a busy day, and I should really get back to it." I was about to take off when I was hit with an idea. It was either incredibly brilliant or incredibly stupid, only time would tell. But once I got it in my head, that wild streak of mine gave me no choice but to act on it. "About that hike," I said, grinning up at Tanner like Connor no longer existed. "I'm swamped today, but if you're free later tonight, maybe we could do dinner?"

His features softened. "I'd like that."

Nerves flooded my system as I felt Connor's gaze

drilling into the side of my face, but I refused to look in his direction. "Great. If you feel like getting away from the lodge for a bit, the Evergreen Diner in town has some of the best food you'll ever eat. I could meet you there. Say . . . seven o'clock?"

"Sounds perfect."

"Awesome." I kept smiling even though my stomach was twisting into knots all of a sudden. "See you then."

I STOOD JUST OUTSIDE THE DINER, STARING IN through the picture windows as a sour taste coated my tongue. I was wrong for using an innocent person like a pawn, and I hated that I'd let my pride take control. Tanner had been nothing but nice, and I felt like a grade-A asshole for taking advantage of that. I might have made questionable decisions, but I wasn't cruel.

"Shit," I hissed under my breath. "Might as well get this over with." I pulled in a breath and prepared to head into the diner to confess to Tanner what I'd done when I heard my name from behind me.

"Ivy." I twisted to look back as he lifted his hand in a wave, that gorgeous smile firmly in place. The man caught the attention of pretty much everyone he passed by as he moved down the sidewalk. "Sorry I'm late. Hope you haven't been waiting long."

God, he was so damn *nice.* My stomach twisted painfully. "You aren't late," I assured him. "I just got here a minute ago."

"Great." His straight white teeth flashed. "Should we head in?" He took a step toward the diner's entrance, his eagerness to get this fake date started as guilt tangled my insides into knots.

"Tanner, wait." Reaching out, I wrapped my fingers around his forearm to stop him. "I need to tell you something."

He tilted his head and looked down at me with curiosity but was otherwise silent, waiting for me to get on with my confession.

"I'm really sorry. I asked you here under false pretenses, and I feel terrible about it."

"Is this about that guy back at the lodge who looked like he wanted to take my head off for talking to you?"

My jaw hinged open. "I—What?"

"That guy. What was his name? Connor?"

I gave my head a brisk shake. "How—I don't . . ." I stopped to clear the frog from my throat. "How did you know?"

One of his massive shoulders lifted in a shrug. "It was impossible to miss. The jealousy wafted off that guy like the stink coming from my gym bag when I've accidentally forgotten it in my trunk for a few days."

I snorted out a laugh at his colorful description while desperately tamping down the strange feeling in my belly his words had stirred to life.

"It's not like that. Believe me, he wasn't jealous." He couldn't have been, not when *he* was the one who snuck out that night. "But things are kind of . . . complicated." My mouth pulled into a wince. "We have history that's kind of embarrassing for me, and I'm ashamed to admit that I asked you here because he was standing there and I was, I don't know, hoping to maybe rile him up or something?" I held my hands up at my sides. "It was childish and a shitty thing to do, and you didn't deserve to be thrown into the middle of it."

Seconds ticked by as he studied me with a measured silence that made me squirm uncomfortably. I was nearly ready to come out of my skin when he finally spoke, and what he said was the last thing I had been expecting.

"I get it. But we're already here and I'm starving, so I say we head inside and eat anyway."

My head jerked back in bafflement. "I—Really?"

"We have to eat, right?" he asked, casual as could be. "I don't see why it should be awkward as long as we go in there with the understanding that it's just two friends having dinner together. I can do that if you can."

"I-I can do that too," I answered, smiling genuinely for the first time in hours as the weight of the shame I'd been carrying around finally drifted away.

"Awesome. Then let's eat. You can make it up to me by telling me what's going on between you and that guy." We started for the glass double doors, only taking a few steps when he stopped and looked back down at me. "Oh, and you should know, your plan totally worked."

My brows dipped down in the middle. "Huh?"

"To rile him up? It worked. I'm surprised smoke didn't start pouring out of his ears."

My heart started to beat faster and my belly swooped. It definitely wasn't the reaction I wanted to have, but I was quickly discovering I had no control over my body when it came to Connor Bennett.

After my confession, dinner went off better than I could have expected, and it wasn't only the awesome food that the crazy old couple who ran the place, Sally and Ralph, cooked. This diner, along with those two, was an institution here in Hope Valley. They'd been around since before I was born, and people liked to say they'd be around long after the rest of us were gone. Sally and Ralph joked that it was all the fighting they did that kept them going.

On top of being incredibly sweet, Tanner was also funny and managed to make me laugh several times throughout our meal. Even when I was sharing all the ugly details of how things went down between Connor and me.

By the end of dinner, Tanner had managed to demolish two slices of Ralph's famous meatloaf, a double helping of mashed potatoes, green beans, and at least half an apple pie. I was full just from watching him.

"Good lord. You really know how to tuck it away, don't you?" I asked with wide-eyed astonishment. "Where the hell does all that food go?"

He wiped his mouth with the paper napkin that had been used to roll his silverware and sat back with a satisfied expression on his handsome face. "All I can eat during the season is grilled chicken and steamed vegetables to stay in shape, so when I get to cheat, I cheat big."

"I'd say," I mumbled.

"You know, while you were talking about everything that went down between you and that cowboy, I got an idea."

I arched a brow in question and sipped some of my iced tea through the straw in my glass. "Oh? And what's that?"

"I think you should take me as a date to the wedding."

I quickly proceeded to choke on the drink I'd just taken. It took several seconds of hacking and wheezing before I could finally breathe again, and Tanner sat there, patiently waiting for me to get my shit together. I hadn't even brought up that my friends had been pressuring me to invite him as my date. He'd come up with the idea all on his own.

"You can't be serious."

"Why not?" He braced his forearms on the table and leaned forward, his face growing serious. "Look, I know nothing's going to happen here," he said, waving a long, thick finger in the space between us. "You made it perfectly clear your head is somewhere else, but I'm a fun guy, and I'm *great* at weddings."

I let out a snort and shook my head with humor. "How can someone be great at weddings?"

He brushed off my question and kept going. "At the very least, you'll have someone to dance with to all the slow songs so you don't have to sit at the table by your-self." Okay, he might have a point there. "And at worst, I can help you make the cowboy green with envy."

I pulled my bottom lip between my teeth. "I don't know," I started hesitantly.

"If you're worried about using me, don't be. I offered myself up this time."

"And I appreciate that, Tanner. I really do," I said, reaching across the table to place my hand on top of his. "But I'm supposed to be moving on, not trying to make an asshole who doesn't even deserve a moment of my time jealous. Not that I'm convinced he would be." Despite what he said earlier, I wasn't sure I bought that Connor got jealous over my interaction with another man. It didn't make sense. He'd clearly been banging his way from rodeo to rodeo after running out of my bed, so why would he be jealous?

"Then we're back to reason number one. You're obviously stressed about having to be in his company for an extended period of time, and it's not like I have anything else to do that night."

I gave him a flat look. "Thanks a lot," I deadpanned.

One corner of his mouth worked its way up in a smirk. "Let me help. I'll make sure you have fun."

I sat back in my booth, giving myself a few moments to mull over everything he'd just offered. "Okay, I'm in."

His eyes brightened. "Really?"

"Yeah. We'll go and have a good time. But you have to give me your word you won't clear the buffet out all by yourself."

"Deal. This is gonna be a lot of fun, Ivy. I promise."

Surprisingly, I was actually starting to believe him.

Chapter Seven

CONNOR

"Dude, what's going on with you?"

I blinked back into the present to find Zach staring at me with a curious look on his face. I'd been so focused on staring at Ivy across the front of the small chapel where my friend and Rae would be exchanging vows tomorrow that I'd completely zoned out mid-sentence of whatever he'd been saying. I couldn't help myself. Any time she was in the room, I couldn't keep from tracking her every move like a heat-seeking missile. When she was close, she was the only thing I was aware of.

As hard as it was, I pulled my attention from the woman I'd been trying to talk to all damn week and looked over to Zach. "What?"

Zach's eye narrowed as he watched me closely. "You didn't hear a damn thing I said, did you?"

I let out a huff of frustration and reached up to pinch the bridge of my nose. "Clearly I didn't, so instead of giving me shit about it, why don't you say it again."

"I asked what's going on with you. You've been acting weird all week."

I cleared my throat, tugging at the collar of my button-down. Rae understood she was dealing with a bunch of cowboys, so she didn't require us to wear suits today since we'd all be stuck in tuxes for the wedding, but she did ask that we at least wear a decent pair of jeans and a nice shirt. Now my throat was starting to feel dry and I felt like the damn thing was choking me. And not the fun, sexy kind of choking either.

"I don't know what you're talkin' about." I didn't know why the hell I decided to lie. It was clear by the look on his face he knew I was full of shit.

"You haven't been yourself, man. You haven't gone out with me and Raylan once since you got here. You've just been hoverin' around the lodge like a lost puppy or something. Hal said he spotted one of the younger female guests hittin' on you, and instead of actin' on it, you just smiled and walked away." He arched a brow, almost in a challenge. "That's definitely not the Connor I know." He sucked in a sharp breath, his eyes going wide. "Christ, are you dying or somethin'?"

"For fuck's sake," I grumbled before remembering that

we were standing in a church and I should probably watch my language. There were already a million reasons why the big guy might strike me down with a lightning bolt or something. I didn't need to give him any more. "No, I'm not dyin', you jackass." Okay, so maybe cleaning up my language was easier said than done. "I just wasn't in the mood." And that was the truth. In fact, I wouldn't have touched that woman with a ten-foot pole if you paid me to. I remembered the chick he was talking about, and I also remembered the ring she'd been sporting on her left hand. When I pointed it out to her after she propositioned me, she'd laughed and made a comment about how she didn't think a guy with my reputation would care about something like that.

She'd been wrong. I had been in the shoes of the guy who was unfortunate enough to put a ring on that woman's finger, and that was a road I would *never* go down.

His eyes nearly bugged out of his head. "Pretty sure *in the mood* is a perpetual state of being for you, brother. You once told me that unless your dick has fallen off, you're good to go."

Fucking hell. In times like this I wished I hadn't leaned so damn hard into the reputation I'd developed over the years. But after all that shit went down with Amber, being the playboy had been the easier choice. I'd tried love. I'd shot for the whole white-picket-fence dream, and I'd been crushed under the weight of it when it all came crashing down.

I figured I was a single man, so why the hell not fuck who I wanted to fuck, consequences be damned. But as I looked across the narthex at the woman I couldn't get out of my head, the regrets started to pile up.

"She was engaged," I told him, my voice low and hard.

"Fuck," he hissed under his breath, reaching up to clap me on my shoulder. "Man, I'm sorry." He knew all about my history with Amber. He'd been there when she and I met, and I'd shared openly with him how I thought she was my endgame. He'd been there when that all imploded and I drowned my sorrows in my buddy Jim Beam for far too long.

"I might be a piece of shit, but there are some lines even I won't cross."

"Hey, knock that shit off," he clipped out, his tone sounding almost angry. "You aren't a piece of shit. Couldn't be, even if you tried. You got your heart stomped on and you decided not to let it happen again. I get why you made that decision. But it doesn't make you a piece of shit."

He might be singing a different tune if he knew what I'd done to Ivy.

And speaking of . . . the main reason I'd been "off" all

week, as he put it, was because of her. That persistent itch beneath my skin that had formed the moment I saw her coming down that staircase hadn't gone away. If anything, it had only gotten worse as the days progressed. The need to see her, talk to her, be in her orbit, was damn near overwhelming. All of the memories of our time together the last time I'd been here came flooding back like a dam bursting. All those lunches we shared out in the meadow covered in wildflowers. All the laughs and fun times. I'd shared things with her I hadn't shared with anyone. She could be stubborn and willful, but she also had the biggest heart of anyone I'd ever known.

I missed her.

I hung around the lodge, hoping for a chance to talk to her, but she seemed to be going out of her way to avoid me at every turn. Just like now. We'd been standing, waiting for the wedding planner to get this rehearsal rolling for a good fifteen minutes now, and she hadn't looked in my direction once. It was like I didn't exist.

I knew she knew I was there because I caught the subtle tensing of her body whenever I got closer and the clenching of her jaw when I first walked in. She might have been doing everything in her power to pretend I wasn't there, but she was just as aware of me as I was of her.

The problem was, she wouldn't give me the goddamn

opening I needed in order to talk to her. I couldn't apologize if she turned and bolted in the other direction every time I got close.

A sharp clap bounced off the tile floors and pulled me from my misery as the wedding planner's cheery voice filled the narthex. "Okay, everyone, we're ready to get started."

I tuned the overly-bright woman out as she rattled on about what we'd be doing this evening. I went through the motions on autopilot, standing up at the altar with Zach's other groomsman, Raylan.

The woman's chirpy voice sounded like it was coming from the opposite end of a long tunnel as I stared across the altar at Ivy, watching her as she focused on the coordinator like she was going to be quizzed on every word the woman said. Her back was arrow straight, her shoulders square and jaw slightly lifted. The only thing giving her away was how tightly she was clasping her hands together in front of her.

We went through the motions of having the girls come up and down the aisle a couple times until everyone felt comfortable. It wasn't until an hour later that I zoned back in when the coordinator instructed us back up the aisle like the ceremony was finally over.

It was obvious from how we were standing that

Lennix would be moving up the aisle with Raylan, while I would be walking with Ivy. I knew there wasn't going to be a more perfect opportunity to talk to her if I conjured it up myself.

My lungs burned as the two of us met at the center of the altar, alerting me to the fact that I had been holding my breath and was in desperate need of fresh oxygen.

"H—" I opened my mouth to speak but managed to choke on the very first letter when my mouth went dry.

At my sputtered cough, Ivy finally looked in my direction for the very first time in days. Her brow was furrowed with concern as she tentatively looped her arm through the crooked elbow I offered her.

"You all right?"

I cleared my throat and spoke, my voice coming out hoarse. "Yeah. I'm good. Sorry about that." I tugged at my collar uncomfortably and tried again as we waited at the top step of the altar for Lennix and Raylan to get a little farther down before we could start across the aisle. "Hi."

She gave me a quick look like I'd grown a horn out of the center of my forehead or something before facing forward as the coordinator waved us on. "Hi," she offered blandly.

I could tell she wanted that to be the end of it, but I couldn't stop myself from saying more. "You look really pretty tonight."

Her head shot back around in my direction so fast it was a wonder she didn't give herself whiplash. "Excuse me?" she asked in a whispered hiss, but there was no missing the displeasure in those two words. It was obvious from her reaction I'd said the wrong thing.

"I said—"

"I heard what you said," she continued with her quiet words, but the anger radiating behind them slammed into me like a rogue wave. "Spare me your empty compliments."

"It wasn't an empty compliment," I insisted, my brows dipping into a frown. I was speaking the God's honest truth. She looked gorgeous tonight. She *always* looked gorgeous.

"I don't want to hear it, Connor." Christ, the sound of my name on her rosy bee-stung lips, even said in that pissed off tone she was using, was enough to rev my engine. What the hell was wrong with me? "Let's just get through this weekend, then we can go back to acting like the other person doesn't exist."

I moved fast when I felt the fingers that had been hugging the bend of my elbow begin to loosen as she attempted to pull away, grabbing hold of her hand with my free one and keeping it firmly in place. I couldn't let her break our connection yet. I knew I had no right to force contact on her like that, but I hadn't realized until she touched me that every breath I'd been taking since those early morning hours when I'd walked out on her had been cut in half. The instant her fingers pressed into the cuffed sleeve of my shirt, my lungs expanded fully for the first time in months. I'd felt like something was missing for so long now, and I'd struggled to put my finger on what it was.

Now I knew.

It was her.

Christ. I'd *really* fucked up.

"I don't want to pretend like you don't exist," I said quietly as the end of the aisle grew closer. "I can't pretend that."

She let out a short, sardonic laugh that felt like a knife to my gut. "I find that hard to believe, considering you've been doing that very thing for months now."

"Butterfly—"

"Don't call me that," she snapped. Her delicate features went hard. Those plump pink lips pulled into a flat line and her cheeks flushed angrily while her slim nose wrinkled at the bridge in disgust. But it was what I saw shimmering in her eyes that stole the air right from my lungs. Pain reflected back at me, radiating so strongly I felt every muscle in my body tense. "You don't get to call me that. Not anymore."

Our friends were only feet away now. "I'm sorry," I

said, those words barely a breath but dripping with dejection as we reached the end of our short journey together. "I'm so fucking sorry, Ivy."

She cast a bewildered look in my direction as I finally released her hand and let it drop from my arm before turning around and walking away.

Chapter Eight

IVY

"You guys ready?" Rae called out from behind the dressing screens in the corner of the bridal suite.

Her big day was finally here, and after we'd all gotten primped and pampered and styled, the time had finally come for her to reveal her wedding gown to all of us. It was the one thing that we, as her bridesmaids, hadn't been a part of. Using connections from her former life, she and her mom had made quite a few trips back and forth to LA to work with a famous designer on Rae's dream wedding dress.

"We're ready," Lennix said impatiently.

A collective gasp sounded through the room once she stepped out from behind the screens. "Oh my God," Lennix breathed as tears welled in her eyes. She hooked arms with her mother, Rory, who was standing behind her, and the two of them held each other up as they took in the woman who was about to become an official member of their family. Not that she wasn't already. "You look so beautiful."

Rae's mother, Alma, stood off to the side with her clasped hands held in front of her smiling mouth. Pride shone in her eyes as she took in her daughter.

"You really do," I said, standing from the dusky pink velvet divan and moving toward her to pull her into a hug. "Zach is going to lose his mind when he sees you in this," I said as I released her and took a step back to take her in once more.

She swished the skirt of her flowing lace gown back and forth, worrying her bottom lip between her teeth. "You really think so? I just want him to like it."

"Honey, you look like a fairy princess," Alma told her.

Rory nodded and sniffled. "Absolutely breathtaking. He's going to love it."

Moving to the champagne bucket beside the vanity, I grabbed an empty glass and filled it up, handing it over to the bride since the rest of us were already set. "Here, drink this. It'll help with your nerves."

She turned her head, smiling a euphoric smile I'd never seen her wear before. It was the smile of a woman who had every single one of her dreams come true. "I'll drink it because I never pass on champagne, but I'm not nervous." She sipped daintily, mindful of her lipstick. "It's strange actually. I was so sure I'd be a huge bundle of nerves today, but I just feel ready. Like this is exactly what's supposed to be happening and Zach is exactly who it's supposed to be happening with. I've never been so sure of anything in my whole life. Is that weird?"

Alma beamed at her daughter as she reached up to gently brush a silky curl over her bare shoulder. "It's not weird at all. It's exactly how I felt when I married your father."

"And it's what I felt when I married Cord," Rory confessed. "Like a piece clicking into place you didn't realize was missing, but as soon as you have it, you know what it means to feel whole."

"Yeah," Rae said on a dreamy sigh. "That's what it feels like."

I forced my lips to stretch into a smile as my stomach dropped to my feet. It wasn't that I was jealous, exactly. I was over the moon that my friends had been lucky enough to meet the loves of their lives, and I wished them decades of happiness to come. But I would have been lying if I didn't feel a small pang of envy at what she was describing. All my life I had wanted a love like that for myself. It was the same kind of love I saw every time I looked at my mom and stepdad. I loved my father. He'd never been anything but good to me, but I wasn't naïve. My mom kept the truth from me until I was old enough to start asking questions, but I knew he'd been a shitty husband. He hadn't been good enough for her, so it made the fact that she found Micah once we moved to Hope Valley even more special.

I wanted that.

And there had only been one time in all my life where I actually felt like I might have found it. Which was why it hurt so damn bad when he ran out on me.

I caught Lennix watching me from the corner of my eye and quickly schooled my features into a false mask of serenity, but I had a feeling from the way she was examining me so closely I hadn't been fast enough.

Noticing the champagne bottle was empty, I quickly snatched it up and gave it a quick shake. "Looks like we've kicked this one. I'm going to grab another bottle real quick. We still have a bit of time before this show gets started."

"Thank you," Rae said happily as I started for the door.

"Hold up." Lennix's voice pulled me up short. "I'll go with you."

Damn it.

I barely made it halfway down the hall before the click

of Lennix's heels caught up with me. "Okay, woman. Start talking."

I made a face I hoped didn't look as fake as it felt as I swung into the tiny kitchen at the back of the church. "What are you talking about?"

She narrowed her eyes like she could see right through me. "Don't give me that. You know exactly what I'm talking about. You got all sad when they were talking about love and happily-ever-afters and stuff." She pointed her finger at my face. "And don't bother denying it, I saw it all over your face."

I bent to yank open the door to the minifridge where I'd stashed a couple extra bottles of champagne earlier. I pulled out the bottle, letting the chill on the glass seep into my palms. "Look, it's really not a big deal, okay? And I don't want to get into it now. This day is all about Rae and Zach. I don't want to take anything away from that."

Her charcoal brows lifted high on her forehead. "You won't take anything away from them by talking to me about what's bugging you. You've been off since last night. You got all quiet during the rehearsal dinner, and that's not like you. Is it about that Tanner guy you came with today?" Her spine shot straight. "Did he do something? I'll kill him."

"No, God. It's nothing like that." I leaned back against the edge of the counter, letting the stone keep me propped up as I heaved out a sigh and rubbed at the tension headache starting to build in the center of my chest. "I slept with Connor," I blurted, deciding it was best to just get it out there. Like ripping off a Band-Aid.

Lennix's jaw dropped wide open, her eyes bugging out so wide it was almost comical. "Last night?" she squeaked.

"No. Not last night. A few months ago, when he was here. Actually, it was the same night he left."

Her eyes went from wide to narrow in confusion. "What do you mean, the same night he left?"

I threw my hands up at my sides and let them drop back down heavily, banging the champagne bottle against the side of my thigh. "I mean I slept with him, and when I woke up, he was gone."

"You're *kidding*."

"I wish I was."

"Oh my God," she hissed, casting a quick glance at the opened doorway behind her to make sure no one was listening before she took three quick steps in my direction, lowering her voice to a whisper. "Why didn't you tell me?"

"I didn't tell anyone," I admitted. "Having the last guy I slept with steal off in the middle of the night wasn't exactly an ego boost. I was humiliated. I didn't want to have to rehash it all."

"I can't believe you slept with *Connor*," she yelped loud enough that I had to shush her. The last thing I needed was for someone to walk down the hall and over-hear our conversation. She dropped her voice back down and added, "And I can't believe that asshole bailed on you in the middle of the night." Her brows pinched together angrily. I knew that look. It was the look that said she was about to rip someone a new asshole.

"Please don't tell anyone," I said quickly, placing the bottle on the counter and clasping my hands in a pleading gesture. "I'm begging you, Lenny. Please keep this to yourself. I don't want anyone else to know."

She rushed forward, taking my hands in hers. "Honey, you have nothing to be embarrassed about. You didn't do anything wrong."

I let out a short scoff. "I'm not so sure about that. I slept with a notorious playboy and was stupid enough to think something might actually come of it. I mean, come on, Len. The guy hasn't exactly hidden the fact that he doesn't do relationships."

Her features softened as worry filled her gaze. "That's why you looked so sad back there, isn't it? You really felt something for him?"

I nodded, having to swallow down the massive lump that had formed in my throat before I could get the words out. "I did. I felt something big. I thought . . ." That ball of sadness was proving harder to dislodge than I'd hoped. "I thought we could be something like Rae has with Zach and your mom has with your dad. I wanted what my mom has with Micah, and I let myself start to see a future with him. Like I said, I was an idiot."

"No, you weren't," she said fiercely before yanking me into a hug so tight it made my ribs creak. "You weren't an idiot. I know you, Ivy, I know the only way you'd ever fall for a man that strongly is if he did everything he could to earn it."

She wasn't wrong. We'd been friends before anything else. At one point, I considered him one of my closest friends. We saw each other nearly every single day when he'd been staying at the ranch. It wasn't like I'd jumped into something quickly. It happened naturally over time. Like we'd been building up to something for months before anything romantic ever happened.

"It doesn't matter anymore." I lifted my shoulders in a heavy shrug. "It's done. Nothing is ever going to happen there, so I just need to move on."

Lennix huffed out a breath and shook her head. "I want to skin that asshole alive for what he did."

I couldn't help but smile at her fierce loyalty. She might have been a few years younger than I was, but she was one of the best friends a woman could ask for. "I love you, but there's really no reason for you to resort to violence."

She harrumphed. "Agree to disagree."

I shook my head on a chuckle. "Seriously, it's okay. *I'm* okay. Just . . . keep this between us. Please? I want to forget any of it ever happened."

"Deal," she agreed. "But I reserve the right to punch him in the dick if he does anything else to hurt you."

"I can give you that."

"But, Ivy, honey, you have to know that it's his loss. You're a total catch. You're beautiful and smart and funny, and you're just the right amount of crazy."

I snorted out a laugh, the fist that had been squeezing my chest in its tight grip the past few hours finally loosening. It was amazing what good friends could do. "How can anyone be the right amount of crazy?"

She shrugged, lifting her hands so her palms faced the sky. "I don't know, but you manage to pull it off."

"Thank you," I said, my voice quiet and sincere. "For letting me talk to you and for having my back. It really helped."

She smiled at me and reached out to give my arm a squeeze. "You never have to thank me for having your back. It's something I'll always do. Now what do you say we take that bottle back and make a huge dent before the ceremony? Then we'll hit the open bar once the reception starts and tie one on. Sound good?"

It sounded perfect.

Chapter Nine

IVY

Lennix and I had done exactly what she'd suggested, taking full advantage of the open bar at the reception.

I couldn't remember a time in the past few months when I'd been this relaxed. A lot of that had to do with the booze, but it was also the atmosphere.

The music was pumping up through the dance floor, making my body vibrate like a live wire as I moved to the fast beat of the song the DJ was playing. A soothing breeze blew in from the fields beyond the massive tent Zach and Rae had set up on the ranch for the reception, moving through the opened walls and caressing my fevered skin. I wasn't sure how long I'd been dancing, but it was long enough that a light sweat had formed at my hairline and the back of my neck.

Everyone was having a great time. My two friends were over the moon now that they were husband and wife. I was surrounded by friends and family, and the buzz I'd been working on since before the wedding was still going strong, working its way into full-on drunk.

The hours had passed without any drama, and I was beyond grateful. Tanner had been right. He was great at weddings. It wasn't awkward for him, being surrounded by so many strangers. I went about making introductions when we first got to the reception, and he was surprisingly good at remembering names. He was able to mingle like he'd been a part of the fabric of this town for years, not only a couple weeks. He kept up with me on the dance floor without complaining.

He was still a big attraction to a lot of the people in town—who the hell knew there were so many hockey fans in Hope Valley—so there were several times throughout the night when he'd been pulled into different conversations that had nothing to do with me, and he held his own perfectly. More than once he'd been caught up in a totally different group than I was, and it was really nice not having to babysit him all night long or make sure he was having a good time.

And speaking of my hot hockey date . . . I spun around when I felt the heat of his large hand land on my shoulder as the song I was dancing to ended and another slower one started up.

"Hey," I chirped happily. Okay, so maybe I had already crossed the line well into drunk, but I was beyond worried about what the hangover would be like in the morning.

He chuckled as he smoothly shifted us into position for a slow dance. One large palm rested on the center of my back—a respectful distance from my ass—and he held my much smaller hand in the other. "Hey back. You look like you're having a good time."

I draped my free arm over his wide shoulder and let my body go lax, allowing him to set us to swaying to the beat. "I'm having a great time. You were right. You're a terrific wedding date."

His grin was big and comforting, and I could see why women all over town were talking about him. There was a part of me that still thought it was a shame I wasn't attracted to him, but there was an even bigger part that was happy to have made a new friend—someone as cool as Tanner Fine. I didn't know if it was a friendship that would extend beyond his vacation to my little town, but I was happy to have met him.

"Thanks. You aren't so bad yourself."

"So, you've been having fun?"

"I really have." He cast a glance around the tent. "Though it seems like things are starting to die down."

I followed his gaze, noticing for the first time the tent was far emptier than it had been at the start of the night. I shouldn't have been surprised. We'd all seen Zach and Rae off hours ago. They were staying at a hotel in the city for the night and flying out for their tropical honeymoon in the morning.

"Oh wow. You're right." I'd been in my own little drunken world and hadn't noticed the party was drawing to a close. The bartender was starting to pack things up and the caterers were clearing the tables of stray dishes and tablecloths. "I'm so sorry." I turned back to Tanner and tilted my face upward. "You were probably ready to go a while ago, and I've dragged it out."

He removed a few strands of hair that had gotten stuck in my lip gloss and tucked them behind my ear. The move was affectionate, but in a friendly way. Once we set that boundary, he hadn't tried to cross it, which I was grateful for. "Not at all. I've had a great time tonight." His eyes traveled to something behind me and the smile on his face turned a bit wicked. "Even with the daggers a certain cowboy has been glaring into my back all night long."

"*What?*" I squeaked out. I tried to whip around, but Tanner held me firmly in place. "Ah ah ah. Don't look. Keep acting like you don't notice he's there; it'll drive him even crazier."

My chest tightened and I started to feel short of

breath. Now that Tanner had mentioned him, I could practically feel Connor's eyes drilling into the back of my head. The desire to turn around and look at him was so strong I had to bite my lip to keep from giving in.

Part of the reason I drank so much tonight was to dull the feel of his eyes tracking me as I moved through the reception. I would have been lying if I said I hadn't noticed him. It was impossible not to. If the man looked incredible in a pair of jeans and a simple T-shirt, it was nothing compared to how good he looked in a tux. He rocked the holy hell out of it. My skin flushed and my blood heated at the first look I got of him before traveling south and centering low in my belly. If I needed proof that I was still as attracted to him today as I had been the first time I laid eyes on him, the way my nipples firmed into tight peaks at the sight of him in that sleek suit was more than enough.

The entire time I stood at the altar while Zach and Rae said their vows, I'd been staring at the man out of the corner of my eye. While Lennix and I wore beautiful satin dresses the color of autumn leaves, Rae had chosen black on black for the men, complete with classic bow ties. The woman might have taken to ranch life like she was made for it, but her sense of style hadn't faded. Zach, Ray, and Connor looked amazing. *Especially* Connor, as much as I hated to admit it.

I'd managed to push the man out of my head with

enough dancing and booze, but now that Tanner brought him up, my whole body tingled with awareness.

"I-is he looking?"

Tanner's eyes glinted with mischief as they came back to me. "Sweetheart, that man's been staring all night long."

I squeezed my eyes closed, pulling in a wobbly breath. I suddenly felt out of sorts, and I didn't know what the hell to do about it. "It's really late," I said quietly as the final strains of the song we were dancing to filled the tent. "We should probably go."

He studied my features, most likely examining my level of intoxication. "You need me to drive you home?"

I smiled up at him with appreciation. "Thanks, but I could actually use a bit of fresh air. I think I'm gonna go for a walk. I'll order an Uber when I'm ready to head home." At the skeptical arch of his brow, I added, "We might be a small town, but we still have ride-shares." I widened my eyes dramatically. "We also have DoorDash and Instacart."

"I believe you, but are you sure it's safe for you to go wandering around by yourself? It's dark, and you've been drinking."

I placed my hand on his chest in a reassuring gesture. "I know this ranch like the back of my hand. Maybe even better. And I'm only heading out to the barn to see the animals. I like to do that to decompress."

The lines that had formed around his eyes and mouth smoothed out as the concern melted from his expression. "Okay. If you're sure."

"I'm positive. Thank you so much for coming with me tonight. I really did have a great time."

"I did too, sweetheart." He hooked my arm through the crook of his elbow and slowly led me out of the tent. "I have an early flight tomorrow, so I probably won't see you before I head out. I just want to tell you that I'm really glad I got to meet you. These two weeks were exactly what I needed. The lodge and this town were the breath of fresh air I'd been looking for, and getting to know you made my time here even better."

I used my hold on his arm to pull him to a stop and lifted up on the toes of my strappy heels to press a kiss to his cheek. "I'm really glad I met you too, Tanner, and I hope you come back any time you need another breath."

"Oh, I have a feeling I'll be back," he said as I used my thumb to swipe off the gloss I'd left behind on his cheek. "Take care of yourself, Ivy Young."

"You too, Tanner Fine. Don't go getting yourself killed next season. I think you've turned me into a bit of a hockey fan, and I'll be severely disappointed if something happens to my favorite goalie."

"Yes ma'am." He let loose a warm chuckle as he took a

step back. "Get home safe, okay?" he requested as he tucked his hands in the pockets of his slacks.

"I will. I promise."

I stood in place, watching as he turned on the heel of his shoe and started in the direction of the lodge. It didn't take any time at all for his big frame to get swallowed up by the dark night, and once it did, I spun in the other direction toward the barn.

There was something about it that comforted me. The sounds and the smells of the animals was calm and familiar. I didn't mind the manure. It was impossible to work on a cattle ranch—even at a fancy lodge like Second Hope—and not get a whiff of manure at least once a day. I barely noticed it anymore.

The lights inside the barn shone brightly like a beacon in the darkness. The stalls that lined both sides of the huge structure were filled with horses, all of them tucked in for the night. I petted the noses of the ones that poked their heads over the stall doors out of curiosity as I moved through, my heels clacking against the hard ground. I made it to the doors at the back and pushed one open, setting off a loud creek that disturbed the otherwise peaceful silence.

While I liked the horses, the animal I liked to visit the most was an ornery goat named Gretel. Most people gave her a wide berth since she was known to try and take a chunk out of your ass if you got close enough, but she and I seemed to have a kind of kinship she didn't have with anyone else. I think we understood each other. I accepted her as the asshole she was and didn't try to change her, so she tolerated me.

"Hey there, pretty girl," I cooed once I reached her. I braced my arms on the top rung of her wooden pen and stared in at her. The other goats were all curled up asleep, but it was almost like she knew it was me walking through the barn so she got up to greet me.

She came up to the railing and bleated loudly, butting her head against the palm of my hand when I reached through. Her way of demanding pets. I was more than happy to comply.

"Did you have a good night?" I asked like the animal would suddenly develop the gift of gab and answer back. I knew it was ridiculous to stand here and talk to a goat, but I liked these little one-sided conversations. Her silence made it possible for me to come up with her responses. Gretel and I had some great conversations this way. She *always* said what I wanted to hear.

"Yeah, I had a good night too. Surprisingly. But you know what they say . . . when in doubt, get drunk," I finished on a giggle

The air around me suddenly grew thick, crackling with a familiar energy that could only mean one thing. I didn't have to look to know who'd just entered the barn. Every single neuron in my body sensed him, and like a magnet being drawn to its partner, I had no choice but to turn around.

Chapter Ten

CONNOR

It had taken everything in me not to get completely shit-faced during the reception after what I overheard earlier that day at the church before the wedding.

The conversation between Ivy and Lennix had been playing on a constant loop in my head all damn night, and I couldn't get it to stop.

I wasn't sure if I'd chosen the right moment or the wrong one to take a piss earlier, but either way, now I knew everything she'd been feeling all these months I'd gone radio silent, and if I hadn't already hated myself, I sure as fuck did now.

"Honey, you have nothing to be embarrassed about. You didn't do anything wrong."

Ivy made a scoffing sound that was anything but

happy. *"I'm not so sure about that. I slept with a notorious playboy and was stupid enough to think something might actually come of it. I mean, come on, Len. The guy hasn't exactly hidden the fact that he doesn't do relationships."*

Lennix's voice had gone gentle. *"That's why you looked so sad back there, isn't it?"*

Hearing that she was sad flayed me right open.

"You really felt something for him?"

"I did. I felt something big. I thought . . ." My stomach plummeted to the floor as I waited for her to finish. *"I thought we could have something like Rae has with Zach and your mom has with your dad. I wanted what my mom has with Micah, and I let myself start to see a future with him. Like I said, I was an idiot."*

I couldn't stand that I'd hurt her. That I made her feel like a fool. Because the truth was, everything she'd been feeling, I felt too. It was why I ran. It scared the shit out of me to feel that way for someone else again. The only thought that had been going through my mind as I slipped out of her bed before the sun had started to come up and got dressed as quietly as possible, was that I couldn't go down that road again. First Dusty, the man I'd held up on a pedestal, tossed me aside. Then Amber broke my heart. Losing the two of them had crushed me. That had been a dark time in my life. But I knew it would have been so much worse to lose Ivy. In the years I'd been with Amber I'd never felt even half of what Ivy made me feel.

I left her before she could leave me because there was no chance I would survive that.

After hearing what I heard, having to watch her dance the night away with that fucking giant nearly drove me to the brink of insanity.

A tiny voice in the back of my head kept telling me to get the hell out of there, that I was torturing myself by sticking around just so I could watch her like a fucking creeper, but I couldn't. I had to see this through, because if she went back to that asshole's room, I was going to have to rip his goddamn head off. As it was, I wanted to break every bone in his hand for touching her all night long.

That dress she'd been wearing had left me in a constant state of arousal. There was nothing more confusing that being pissed off and sporting a hard-on at the same time. So much of the blood in my body was centered in my dick that I felt lightheaded. The copper color of her dress looked perfect against her creamy skin and made the rose-gold shade of her hair shine like it was about to catch fire. When she turned at the end of the aisle to take her place and I saw the only thing covering her back were two flimsy straps that crisscrossed all the way down to those sexy little dimples above her ass, I went hard enough to pound nails, and it never let up. It was a wonder I'd been able to function at all.

Knowing Tanner *Fucking* Fine got to spend the whole night feeling all that silky-smooth skin when they danced drove me crazy. Every time he touched her hair, tucking those strands behind her ear, I wanted to kill him.

The level of intensity and consistency that I continued to watch them with was bordering on disturbing, but I couldn't make myself stop. When they started walking out of the tent it felt like someone punched right through my chest and was squeezing my lungs in an iron fist. My feet moved with no instruction from my brain whatsoever, taking off after them. I didn't have the first clue what the hell I was doing or how I could possibly stop them from leaving together. I only knew I had to do *something*.

I watched from a safe—albeit stalker-ish—distance as the two of them stopped a few yards outside the tent. I thought I was going to ground my molars into dust when she lifted up on the toes of those fucking heels and kissed his cheek.

I watched with bated breath as the two of them talked for minute, but then, to my unbelievable relief, the giant jackass started backing away, and a minute later, the two of them headed off in separate directions.

Blowing out the gust of breath I'd been holding in my

lungs, I set into action, following Ivy at a distance as she started off for the barn while Tanner headed back toward the lodge. I knew exactly where she was headed. She once told me that when she needed to clear her head or take a break from people, she liked to go out to the goat pen. For some reason that crazy woman's favorite animal on the whole ranch was a psychotic goat with crazy eyes that tried to physically maim everyone it came across. For some reason, I couldn't help but think that was so perfectly her.

Of course the wild little butterfly would connect with a psycho goat.

I could hear the smoky cadence of her seductive voice coming from out back as I moved down the alleyway between the horse stalls, but it was too far to make out the words. I paused just inside the open barn door, trying to figure out what the hell I was going to say.

My heart was beating in my ears so hard it was a wonder I could hear anything beyond that, but the shuffle of footsteps on the ground just outside managed to break through. A second later she stepped through the opening into the barn, that fresh lemon and basil scent of hers filling the air and erasing other harsher smells all around us completely. Or maybe it was just because I was aware of every single little thing about her to the point of obsession.

Her heels clicked slowly across the dusty concrete floor

as she came into view. Those sapphire eyes landed on me a second later, not an ounce of surprise on her beautiful face, like she'd already known I was there. Her cheeks held a rosy glow, her skin looking dewy and soft, even under the harsh overhead lights.

The woman was incapable of looking bad, no matter what. I was willing to bet she'd still take my breath away on day three of the flu. She could look like an extra on *The Walking Dead* and I would still want her.

Ivy stood opposite me across the alleyway, her back pressed against the rough wood of the stall, her arms crossed over her chest, pushing her tits up. It was nearly impossible for me not to stare, but somehow I managed to keep my gaze above her neck.

"What are you doing in here?"

"I—" I thought about lying but quickly decided that would be the wrong move. I needed to start making things right. I couldn't do that if I lied. "I saw you come in here."

Her brows rose high on her forehead. "And . . . what? You followed me?"

"Yes," I answered plainly. "I saw you heading in here and I followed you."

She scoffed, giving her head a shake and pushing off the wall. I moved quickly, panic setting in when she started for the exit. I closed the space between us in two steps and wrapped my fingers around her bicep to stop her. "Ivy, please."

Her head shot around, her eyes narrowing in on where I was touching her. I snatched my hand back as soon as I realized I was touching her without permission. "Please," I said, holding them up in surrender. "I only want to talk. I want to try and explain."

She let out a bark of caustic laughter. "You really think there could ever be an explanation that I would want to hear?"

I didn't, but that didn't mean I wasn't going to try. "I thought I was doing the right thing. For you."

Her head fell back, a humorless smile that didn't belong on her beautiful face stretching across her mouth. "What a fucking cop-out."

"It's not a cop-out," I insisted, that pressure in my chest increasing by the second. She had to understand. I had to *make* her understand. It was the only way I could fix what I fucked up. "Look, I know it sounds like bullshit, but I swear, the only thing going through my head when I took off on you was that you deserved better. That night . . ." My mouth suddenly felt like it was stuffed full of cotton. I tried swallowing but there was no relief. "That night, the things I felt . . . I wasn't prepared. I know what I did was fucked up, and it's not an excuse, but I was scared.

I knew I couldn't give you what you deserved. I'd wanted you for so fucking long, but after we—"

"Fucked," she clipped out, wrapping her arms over her chest, the gesture more protective than anything, like she was trying to give herself a hug, almost. "That night, after we fucked."

That night had felt like so much more than that. Than just a fuck. So to hear her boil it down to its root parts felt like a slap in the face. A well-deserved one, sure, but it still fucking hurt.

"I knew I wasn't good enough for you. I'm *not* good enough for you. But there hasn't been a single day that's passed since I left that I haven't thought about you. I can't get you out of my head." I was making a mess of this whole thing. But I didn't know how the hell to put into words everything I had been feeling that night—what I was feeling in that moment. It was like the more I tried to explain, the worse I was making it.

I scrubbed my hands over my face with a groan, raking my fingers through my hair in frustration. "Christ, I'm not saying any of this right."

"No, you're really not," Ivy said dryly. "And I'm done listening. I don't want to hear anymore bullshit excuses or watered-down apologies. As far as I'm concerned, it was a mistake. End of story."

Dread made my heart rate slow and my brain short-circuit so I wasn't thinking when she started away from me. All I could do was act—desperate to do anything that would get her to stay. My hand shot out just as she started to pass me, wrapping around the back of her neck and propelling her back around. She stumbled on her heels, but I was there before she could fall, letting her crash into my chest to keep her upright before slamming my lips down on hers. The kiss wasn't soft or graceful. It was full of every ounce of need that had been clawing at my insides since I walked away months ago. I swiped across the seam of her lips with my tongue, begging for entry, and when they parted on a surprised gasp, I didn't hesitate to dive inside.

With one hand tangled in the hair at the nape of her neck, I tipped her head back and plundered. Adrenaline dumped into my bloodstream like a dam breaking. My dick was so goddamn hard I could feel my pulse in it.

When she finally pulled away several seconds later, we were both breathing like we'd just sprinted a mile uphill in the heat of the day. I stood, waiting for whatever her reaction might be. I had no right to kiss her, and I fully expected her to slap the shit out of me for taking such liberties, but I hadn't been able to help myself. It was like trying to survive without breathing.

Impossible.

"What happened between us wasn't a mistake," I

panted, the breaths sawing in and out of my lungs. "I fucked it up. I ruined everything, but it wasn't a mistake."

My words spurred her into action. One moment she was standing across the alleyway from me, her eyes wide and glassy, her delicate fingers held over her lips in shock, and the next she was lunging for me.

Chapter Eleven

CONNOR

Her smell enveloped me as we crashed together once more in a kiss even hungrier than the last. That fresh lemon and basil had become my favorite scent long ago, and as my tongue ravaged Ivy's mouth, tangling and twisting with her own, I tried to breathe in as much of it as I possibly could. I tasted the bitterness of the vodka and tonic water and the citrus of the limes from the vodka tonics she'd been drinking all night. That was her go-to cocktail: vodka tonic with two limes squeezed into it. It was one of the many things I'd learned about her during all those months we'd been friends. During those months I'd been heading down a path I'd sworn to myself I wouldn't go down again.

The blood pumping in my ears sounded like white-water rapids but I still managed to hear the greedy little whimpering sounds Ivy made that I gladly swallowed down. Her hands fisted the lapels of my tuxedo jacket, using her iron grip to keep me close as she rose up on the toes of those sexy-as-fuck heels to take the kiss deeper.

A growl worked its way up my throat as I gripped her hair, wrapping it around my fist and using it to tug her head back so I could drag my tongue down the column of her throat. I nipped at her collarbone before traveling back upward, stopping to take my time at the spot right beneath her ear that drove her absolutely wild.

A low, throaty moan slipped past her lips as she dropped her head farther back, giving me better access. From our night together, I knew that spot was one of her buttons, and it might have made me an asshole to jab on it right then, but I wasn't above playing dirty. I teased and kissed and licked until she was panting for air. I dragged my teeth along the cord of her throat and kissed my way down, down, down to that tantalizing dip in the neckline of her dress that had been driving me crazy all goddamn night.

I sucked at the skin across her chest just above the swells of her round tits, leaving red marks along her cleavage.

"Mmm, Connor," she hummed, lifting her head. Her pupils were blown, the black swallowing up so much of that crystal blue that there was only a small rim around the very edge. Her cheeks were rosy with want, her lips swollen from my own. Her gaze was hazy as she blinked her hooded eyes at me.

"What do you want, butterfly?" I rasped. I banded one arm around her waist, holding her to me as tightly as possible. I grabbed behind her right knee and hiked her leg up to my hip, exposing her thigh from beneath the slit in her dress. I could feel the warmth of her pussy through the layers between us, and it was enough to make my hips buck involuntarily, rubbing my steel erection against her core through our clothes.

She replied by reaching up and gripping my hair, yanking my mouth back down to hers. My tongue thrust against hers in the same rhythm as my hips, my rock-hard cock teasing her clit through her panties. I could feel her wetness seeping through the layers.

"Tell me, Ivy," I demanded, my words gritted out as I slid my hand upward so I could drag the pad of my thumb over her nipple that was puckered hard beneath the slinky material of her dress. My girl wasn't wearing a bra underneath—that much was obvious thanks to the non-existent back—and I could see perfectly that her nipples were painfully hard, begging to be sucked on until what I knew from memory was a soft petal pink turned bright red. "Tell me what you want."

She kept her leg hooked over my hip of her own accord

as she trailed one of her small hands down the front of my shirt, curling her fingers so I could feel the scrape of her nails. Her tongue darted out and licked across my Adam's apple just as her hand reached the waistband of my pants. Before I knew what was happening, she had my fly undone and her hand slid inside, gripping my cock so fast I grunted at the unexpected contact.

Her eyes widened as she looked down. Her hand worked me under my pants and boxer briefs. Her grip exactly how I liked it. She held me in a tight fist, sliding her hand upward and twisting at the crown, gathering the pre-cum that was already leaking out so she could use it to make the glide easier. "God, I nearly forgot how big you are."

"I never forgot," I admitted on a growl. "I still remember how tight your cunt gripped me and how sweet it tasted. I've thought about that every goddamn day for months while I'm fucking my own fist and coming on my stomach."

She blinked once, her eyelids remaining low and sultry as her tongue peeked out and pulled her plump bottom lip between her teeth. "You want me to tell you what I want?"

I dragged my thumb over her nipple once more, eliciting a gasp from her. "*Fuck yes.*"

Her fingers flexed around my length before sliding painfully slowly downward. "I want you to stuff your fingers inside my pussy. I want to jack your big cock while you fuck me with those fingers until you're so crazy you can't stand it for another second." Her hips rolled as she spoke, rubbing herself against me so I could feel the heat from her cunt. She was driving me out of my goddamn mind. "Then I want you to fuck me," she said on a whisper, that tongue sliding out again to flick across my top lip. "Right here in this barn."

My chest vibrated on a primal sound as I reached down and grabbed her by the wrist, pulling her hand out of my pants. "If that's what you want, baby," I said in a low, craggy voice.

Her chin hitched up with determination, her eyes boring into mine. "It is."

"All right then. But if you're gonna jack me off, we need a little somethin' to make it easier." I lifted her hand between us so it was face level, then I worked to unfold her fingers so her palm was flat. "Spit." I ordered.

She blinked. The way her chest stuttered on an exhale and the frantic thrum of the pulse in her neck the only outward signs that my command affected her. She pursed those bee-stung lips and did as I said, spitting into the center of her palm. "Good girl." I didn't waste another second guiding her hand back down and shoving it into my boxers. "Now fuck me with that little fist."

She gave my erection another squeeze, this one almost

too tight, and when I grunted and flinched, she smiled wickedly right before the flutter of pain turned into pleasure. *Fuck, my wild woman.* Those little glimpses had driven me to her in the past and were what kept me panting after her, even all these months later. There was a lot I liked about this woman, but her wild streak had to be right at the top.

I kept my eyes locked on hers while she worked my cock exactly how I liked it and watched her closely as I sucked my index and middle fingers into my mouth. She swallowed thickly, her eyes falling to my mouth as I pulled out the slicked-up digits and moved to slide my hand beneath her skirt. "Fuck, you're so goddamn wet," I grunted as I shoved the lacy scrap of material between her thighs to the side and brushed along her slit. She was practically dripping. "Is this all for me?" I asked as I gathered that wetness up on my fingers and used it while I moved up and began to circle her clit.

Her head tipped backward on a hitched breath, bumping lightly into the wood of the stall wall behind her. "Stop teasing and put them inside me already." Christ, I loved it when her voice got all husky with sex. She could make billions as a phone sex operator if she wanted to.

"Like this?" I didn't give her any warm-up before shoving my two fingers as deep as they could go.

"Oh fuck!" she cried out, her hips lurching forward as

she dropped her head onto my shoulder. Her pussy was as tight as I remembered, locking around my fingers like a vise. I gave her a moment to adjust, but not all the way before pulling out and stuffing her full once more. We might have only had one night together, but it was enough for me to learn what she liked, and my wild little butterfly liked to be fucked rough.

"Is this what you were wanting?" I teased as I fucked her with those two fingers so hard her body jolted against mine. I kept my pace slow, but my strokes nearly brutal, and in no time, her walls were fluttering against me.

"God, Connor, *yes*." Her tits heaved on choppy breaths as we used our hands to fuck each other. My dick was leaking with so much pre-cum I felt the wet spot on the front of my boxer briefs growing bigger by the second. Meanwhile, Ivy was so wet she was dripping down my wrist.

"You ready for a third?" I asked, thumbing her clit as I worked my fingers in and out of her. "Need to stretch you a little wider if you're gonna take my cock, baby."

Her head bobbled on a nod. She sucked in a gasp as I started to work a third finger into her tight, wet, heat. Even as drenched as she was, it was a tight fit.

"Oh shit," she yelped as her hand around my cock started to work in time with each plunge of my fingers. My cock got even harder at the feel of her clenching my fingers, at the sound of her wetness as I fucked her deep, at the smell of her arousal and the noises she made as she fisted my cock, jerking me even faster. Her movements matched my own, and she began to rock on my hand, picking up the pace the closer she got. I wanted to hear and feel her come, but I needed to hold out until I could get inside her.

With my other hand, I reached down and stopped her from taking me any further as I worked her higher and higher.

"Connor, I'm—"

"Do it, Ivy. Come on my hand so you can come on my cock."

Her orgasm washed over her then, her walls clenching and fluttering with her release. I had to grind my teeth together to keep from shooting off at the sound of her. As soon as her release left her, I pulled my fingers free and fisted her panties, ripping them clean off her body and tossing them aside.

"Take my cock out," I commanded as I lifted my hand to my lips and sucked her intoxicating flavor off my fingers.

Her hands worked fast, pulling my dick free and shoving my pants and underwear over my hips. She licked her lips as she eyed it, making it twitch. "You have a condom?" she asked, her eyes pleading.

In short, quick movements I pulled out the one I kept in my wallet and ripped the wrapper open with my teeth. I slid it into place, hoisted her up, and braced one arm under her ass to hold her in place as her legs wrapped around my waist. I lined up the head of my cock with her sopping entrance and nudged it into place.

"Now," she practically begged. "Now, Connor. Please. Fuck me."

My control shattered. With one snap of my hips, I buried myself balls deep in the only woman I'd ever wanted this goddamn badly.

Her jaw hinged open and her eyes bugged out. "Oh fuck!" She sucked in a startled gasp as my cock stretched her wide. "Oh my God."

"Shh," I soothed when she squeezed her eyes closed and curled her lips between her teeth, biting down hard. "It's okay, honey. Just breathe." I brought my free hand up beneath her chin and tilted her face to mine so I could give her a slow, sensual kiss, hoping it would relax her. I began to move slowly when her kisses turned desperate and her hips started to roll, her silent way of urging me on.

"That's it, Ivy." I began sliding in and out, careful not to rush and risk hurting her. "God, you're so beautiful."

She whimpered, her teeth clamping down on her bottom lip as her cunt began to pulse around me.

"More," she demanded on a heavy breath.

I picked the pace up a bit, the feel of her silky clutch slowly killing me, but Christ, what a way to go.

"Connor, more. Stop holding back. I want you to fuck me."

My lips curled back on a growl as I gave her exactly what she was asking for. I drove my cock into her so hard the sound of skin slapping against skin echoed around the barn. Her cries grew louder and sharper. Ivy's nails dug into my scalp at the back of my head as her heels dug into my ass, and the sting of both only spurred me on.

"Yes, just like that," she gasped as her tits bounced with each brutal thrust. Reaching up, I yanked the thin strap of her dress down her shoulder, exposing that pale pink nipple. I cupped her tit and lifted it, wrapping my lips around the stiff peak and sucking hard as I continued to fuck her up against the rough wooden wall.

"Don't stop!" she cried out, gripping my hair in her fists and holding my face to her chest. I made quick work of exposing the other one and giving it the same treatment, abusing her pretty nipples until they glowed blood red and I'd left deep purple marks all over her chest.

I would have gladly suffocated in the valley of her cleavage a very happy man, but I wanted to see her face when she came, and I could feel her getting close.

"That's it, Ivy," I said as I watched her throat work on all the noises she was making. "God, look at you. Look how well you're taking me, baby. See how perfectly your cunt's taking my dick?"

She looked down to where our bodies connected, my cock glistening with her arousal every time I pulled out before slamming back in.

My balls drew up tight against my body as tingles spread beneath my skin. I had to clamp down on the inside of my cheek until I tasted blood to keep from coming. No way was I getting off until she did. "Look at you, taking me like such a good girl."

"Oh fuck, Connor," she said in a high-pitched, pleading tone. "I'm gonna come. Don't stop."

"Fuck yes," I hissed as I lost my rhythm and began slamming into her frantically. "Fuckin' squeeze my cock. Come all over me and milk me dry."

She tossed her head back on a broken cry as she exploded, clamping down around me as she came on a scream of my name. It was impossible to hold off when her pussy was clutching me like a hot, velvet vise. I let loose on a primal roar, pouring into her body, spurt after agonizing spurt. I came so hard stars burst in front of my eyes. I managed to lock my knees before they could give out, staying buried deep as her cries turned into whimpers.

I'd come harder than I had in my entire life, and the only thing I could think was how fucking badly I wanted to do it again.

Chapter Twelve

IVY

My surroundings were pitch black as I blinked my gritty eyes open. My mouth was dry and my brain was foggy as I tried to clear the lingering effects of alcohol and sleep away so I could remember where the hell I was. It came back to me as my eyes adjusted to the darkness well enough to take in my unfamiliar surroundings.

It all came back to me in a rush, crashing into me like a garbage truck filled to the brim in the middle of the hottest day of the year. I realized the heavy weight banded around my ribs was an arm, and I suddenly recalled who that arm belonged to.

After our drunken hookup in the barn, we'd come back to Connor's room at the lodge for two more rounds before I finally passed out from sex and inebriation.

I clenched my thighs at the memory of how thoroughly he'd fucked me, feeling a sharp twinge in my core from the workout it had gotten.

I wish I could claim I was too drunk to know what the hell I'd been doing, but that wouldn't have been true. I had been drunk enough that all my inhibitions were lowered so I was able to say *screw it* and not give a damn about the consequences. And as the night wore on and he forced one orgasm after another from my body, the more sound my mind became. However, by then I felt so damn good I'd decided to just roll with it.

A soft snore came from behind me, the feel of Connor's breath gently brushing against the bare skin of my shoulder bringing me back to the present. We were currently tangled up in his sheets, his massive body the big spoon to my little one. He had me secured to him with that arm and was holding firmly onto my left breast in his sleep.

I tilted my head on the fluffy pillow to get a look at the alarm clock on the bedside table, the glowing white numbers showing it was a quarter after three in the morning. The sun was far from rising. I could have easily put my head back down and gone back to sleep, but there was no way that was happening. I'd had my fun, and now it was time for me to get the hell out. There was no way in hell I was giving Connor Bennett the chance to sneak out on me in the middle of the night *again*.

This time, I was going to be the one to walk out on him.

Holding my breath, I slowly and carefully lifted his arm high enough so I could slide out from under it and off the bed. Once I managed to slither myself onto the floor, I popped my head up over the mattress and looked to make sure he was still asleep. When he still hadn't moved five seconds later I let out a relieved gust of air and pushed to standing, slowly creeping around on my tiptoes as I searched the dark room for my discarded clothing.

I remembered Connor shredding my panties earlier, then picking them up off the dirty barn floor and stuffing them in his pocket on the way out. I hadn't been wearing a bra, so all I needed to find was my dress and heels. The good thing about our little X-rated exercise session was that I was now sober enough to drive myself home and wouldn't have to call on an Uber during my walk of shame. Ride shares here in Hope Valley weren't the same as in a big city. It was more likely than not the car would be driven by someone you knew.

I could imagine how humiliating it would be to get picked up from what was essentially a booty call by my sophomore Lit teacher who was driving to save cash for a beach vacation. Or the sweet receptionist at the local clinic who was helping put her grandkid through college. I was grateful as hell to dodge that particular bullet.

I used the sliver of moonlight coming through the partially opened curtain to untangle my dress and slide it back on. It was probably wrinkled to hell from lying on the floor of Connor's room the past several hours, but all I could do was hope there wasn't anyone lingering in the great room as I snuck out. Hooking the straps of my shoes over my fingers, I reached the door just as Connor shifted in the bed. I stopped in place, my hand on the door handle, my lips curled between my teeth as I stared over the shadowed mass in the bed, praying he didn't wake up.

He stirred for a few more seconds. I thought I was busted when the arm that had been wrapped around me stretched out like he was feeling for me in his sleep, but instead of waking up, he rolled over onto his back and threw that same arm over his eyes. The sheet was pooled at his waist, leaving his defined chest and carved marble abs on full display.

I licked my lips unwittingly as I took a few more moments to appreciate the man's gorgeous body, then I got my shit together and got the hell out of there.

The great room was blessedly quiet as I crept down the stairs to the first floor. The reception desk was shut down and the restaurant and bar were dark and empty. I booked it out to the staff parking lot where I'd parked earlier and moved as quickly to my car as I could, given I was running barefoot on gravel. I practically dove into the driver's seat and threw the car into reverse, finally letting out a sigh of relief when I left the lodge in my rearview mirror.

FROM THE CURIOUS LOOKS I KEPT GETTING FROM everyone who walked into Muffin Top, the most popular coffee and pastry shop in town, I knew I probably looked ridiculous, sitting inside with oversized sunglasses perched on my nose, but the dark lenses were the only thing keeping my head from splitting open.

After I returned home from the lodge, I'd crawled my exhausted ass back into bed and slept for several more hours. I probably could have slept longer, but shortly after eight, a certain angry bull rider showed up on my front porch, beating on my front door and blowing up my cellphone at the same time. Was it cowardly to lock myself in my bathroom and hide until he finally gave up and went away? Maybe. Okay, yes. I was a chickenshit. I kept telling myself that fair was fair. He'd dipped out on me, and I simply returned the favor. I didn't owe him any kind of explanation.

Shortly after he left, Lennix had called asking if I

wanted to meet her for coffee. I wanted to say no and spend the whole day in bed binging true crime documentaries. My hangover was beating at my skull almost as hard as Connor had been beating at my front door, but I knew the odds of him showing back up at some point were high, and it would be easier to avoid the man if I wasn't here. It was only a matter of time before he took off again or got sick of me. I just needed to wait him out, and what better way to do that than with caffeine.

"You look like flattened roadkill," Lennix pointed out lovingly from across the table we'd managed to snag near one of the large windows. Like the Evergreen Diner, Muffin Top was a Hope Valley institution, and it was usually hopping, no matter what time of day it was.

I gave her a flat look behind my sunglasses as I took a much-needed hit from my coffee cup. "Thanks," I deadpanned, holding up my middle finger for her to see.

She let out a tinkling giggle as she pulled off a piece of her chocolate croissant and popped it into her mouth.

"It's just a hangover. I've had more than my fair share in my life. A little more coffee and a bit of grease and I'll be good as new."

"Hmm." She gave me a look that had my hackles rising as she slowly chewed her croissant.

"What?" I began to fidget in my seat as she watched me keenly. "Why are you looking at me like that?"

"Oh, no reason," she said nonchalantly. "I just figured you'd be in a better mood today. You know, since a certain sexy bull rider practically railed you into the barn wall last night."

I choked on the bite of my strawberry cheese Danish I'd just taken and proceeded to hack up a lung.

"Jeez, Ivy." Lennix sputtered out a laugh as she rounded the table, coming over to my side to pound on my back until the food dislodged and I was finally able to pull in a breath. "I just wanted to give you a hard time. Not kill you."

My sunglasses had fallen off at some point while I was choking, and with my eyes uncovered, I shot my friend a bewildered look. "How did—I wasn't—That's not—" I had to stop and suck back another gulp of coffee to soothe my suddenly dry throat. I worked to center myself as Lennix returned to her seat, counting to ten in my head as I inhaled a calming breath before pushing it back out.

"How did you know?" I finally managed to get out, my cheeks so hot I knew they had to be glowing an unnatural shade of red.

"I saw him follow you to the barn," she replied with a casual shrug. I waited a few minutes, but when neither of you came out, I went to check on you. You know, to either make sure you hadn't killed him or to help you dispose of the body. I didn't even make it inside before I . . . *heard*."

I slapped my hands over my face with a pained groan as she waggled her eyebrows at me. "Oh God."

Lennix reached across the table and pulled my hands away. "Hey, knock that off. You didn't do anything wrong. From the sounds of it, you were both doing something *very* right."

"For the love of God," I grumbled, collapsing back in my chair and folding my arms over my chest. "Did you see—?"

Lennix's entire face scrunched up like she'd just sucked on a rotten lemon. "Ew, no! I heard you two going at it and hightailed it out of there." She faked a shiver of repulsion. "Please. I love you, babe, but I do *not* want to see that." She munched on her croissant before speaking around the flaky pastry. "So does this mean the two of you kissed and made up?"

I let out an indelicate snort. "Not a chance in hell." I reached up to massage my aching temples. "It was just a stupid, drunken hookup."

As if to contradict my point, my cellphone started to buzz from my back pocket, and when I pulled it out, Connor's name was flashing across the screen. It was the fifth call I had ignored so far this morning. I quickly mashed the button on the side to send it to voicemail and dropped the phone onto the table in frustration.

Lennix looked from me to the phone and back again,

her brows lifting high on her forehead inquisitively. "That him?"

"Yeah," I said on a sigh, popping another bite of Danish into my mouth. "Guess he wasn't thrilled to wake up this morning and discover I'd taken a page out of his book."

Lennix let out a bubble of surprised laughter. "You mean you bailed on him in the middle of the night?"

I nodded. "Yep. Took off while he was still sound asleep."

"Hell yes, Ivy!" she declared, reaching across the table for a high five. "Way to give that bastard a taste of his own medicine. But I'm curious."

"About?"

"Well . . . how was it?" She leaned in, lowering her voice so only I could hear as she asked, "Is hate sex really as good as people claim it is?"

"God, it really is," I lamented pathetically, scrubbing my hands over my face. "I really wish I could say it sucked, but it was even better than the first time."

Just then, my phone started to vibrate again. I flipped it over so the screen was face down, but I wasn't fast enough.

"Clearly." Lennix let out a knowing chuckle. "Has he been blowing up your phone all morning?"

"Yep," I answered, popping the P obnoxiously as I

finished off my coffee. "But he'll lose interest soon enough. The guy has the attention span of a fruit fly when it comes to women."

She arched a skeptical brow. "You sure about that?"

Of course I was sure. It was how the man operated. "I'm sure. And besides, it's not like he's sticking around. He'll be back traveling the circuit any day now. As soon as those buckle bunnies are in front of him again, I'll be a distant memory."

I might have sounded unaffected by it, but the words left a curdled taste on my tongue and a pinched feeling in my stomach.

I was about to suggest a change of subject when the door to the coffee shop swung open, setting off the bell above it. My attention turned to the woman who'd walked in, my eyes going wide with shock.

I could have sworn the entire shop went quiet as people turned to stare.

"Holy shit," Lennix breathed out on a whisper, having turned to scope out the newcomer at the same time I did.

"Is that—?"

"Blythe Fanning," she answered before I finished my question.

My surprise instantly gave way to sadness as I noticed the two little kids trailing into Muffin Top right behind her and the toddler she had propped on her hip. I'd grown up with Blythe. She was several years older, but on top of this being a small town, our parents were close friends, so we knew each other well enough. She'd left for college when she was eighteen, and instead of coming back when she graduated, she married the guy she'd been dating since her freshman year and ended up moving to where he was from.

I knew her mom, Nona, and stepfather, Trick, had missed her tremendously, but as long as she was happy, they were happy.

"Sunny said she'd spoken to her recently, but didn't mention anything about her moving back," Lennix said quietly. When I looked back to her I noticed she was wearing the same expression of sadness I was.

"Makes sense. With three kids?" I gave my head a shake of disbelief. I couldn't possibly imagine how hard things had been for her lately. "I'm sure she needs help."

"God, it's just so sad," Lennix said, putting to words exactly what I was feeling. "My heart's broken for her."

Instead of being rowdy or noisy, the kids were quiet, their heads down and shoulders scrunched up to their ears. Grief was pouring off the little family in waves.

Just then, Blythe turned from where she'd been placing an order at the counter and caught sight of us, offering a smile that barely shifted her lips. There was no missing the dark rings beneath her eyes or the pallor of her skin. Her hair was flat and dull. She looked exhausted and weary and heartbroken.

With her children still I tow, she started toward our table. "Hey, guys," she offered congenially enough once she reached us.

"Hey, sweetie." I quickly stood, wrapping her in an embrace, noticing her bones stood out more prominently than they should have. She returned the hug with a pat to the back and I stepped away so Lennix could do the same.

"It's so good to see you," she offered the woman who looked like the shine had been snuffed right out of her.

"It really is. We didn't know you were back."

She cleared her throat and ran a hand over her hair, the gesture almost nervous, like she was realizing for the first time that she wasn't at her best. "Uh, yeah. It was kind of unexpected."

I smiled, hoping it would put her at ease. "Of course. Anyway, it's great to have you here. I'm sure your mom is happy." Every word out of my mouth felt pathetic and trite, but I didn't know what I could possibly say to make the situation any better. What did you say to a woman whose husband died unexpectedly, leaving her and their three little ones with a gaping hole in their lives? I couldn't imagine the pain she must have been feeling. It was written over every single inch of her.

"She is. Thanks."

The barista behind the counter called her name, breaking the awkward tension that was surrounding us. "Well, that's me. I should probably get going," she said as the little girl on her hip began to fuss. "It's nap time anyway. But it was good to see you guys."

"You too," Lennix returned.

"And if you need anything, we're just a phone call away, all right? Anything you need. Just name it."

She sniffled, her smile wobbly but more genuine that time around. That was something, at least. "Thanks. I really appreciate that."

She and her kids left a few moments later, and as soon as the door closed behind them, a low din started up throughout the coffee shop. People began to whisper and speculate about the recent widow and her poor kids.

It was bad enough having to suffer through the loss she'd experienced, but I couldn't imagine coming back to the town where I'd grown up to have everyone gossip about me behind my back.

I made a silent vow right then that I was going to do better than the other busybodies in town. I was going to try and be the kind of friend Blythe needed.

Chapter Thirteen

IVY

"Are you all right, love bug? You're looking a little green."

I stumbled out of eagle pose at my mom's question and lowered myself to my mat as a wave of dizziness washed over me. I closed my eyes and inhaled deeply, pulling in the fresh air and the sweet perfume of the plants and flowers that surrounded me into my lungs. I took slow, centering breaths as I tried to push away the nausea gripping my stomach.

When my mom, Hayden, had called earlier this morning and asked if I wanted to do yoga, I'd invited her over, hoping that a little bit of exercise would help get my energy back up. I'd been feeling run down lately thanks to a nasty stomach virus that didn't seem to want to go away.

"Yeah," I blew an exhale past my lips as the worst of the

nausea passed. "I'm good." I peeled my eyes open and looked at my mother, offering her a smile. "This bug is just kicking my ass. It doesn't want to go away."

She lowered onto her mat beside mine and leaned over to place her palm on my forehead as her brow furrowed. "You aren't running a fever," she said, but she didn't sound relieved by that knowledge.

"I'm fine, Mom. Really."

She still looked skeptical, and I knew she was fighting her desire to go full-on helicopter mom like she had whenever I'd been sick as a kid. It wasn't something that happened very often, but when it did, it never failed to knock me on my ass. "If you say so. Just promise me that if you don't get any better in a few days you'll go see the doctor."

"I promise. But it's really not necessary." I grabbed my water bottle from the grass beside me and popped the top, gulping some back. "See? I'm already feeling better."

She hummed but let it go.

Giving up on more yoga, I let myself fall back onto my mat and stared up at the fat white clouds that dotted the bright blue sky. "You can keep going if you want," I told her. "I'm going to lie here and pick out shapes in the clouds."

Instead of flowing into her next pose, my mother stretched out on the ground beside me. "I forgot all about your cloud picking. You learned that from Sylvia, didn't you?"

"Yeah. She and I used to spend hours lying out here, finding all kinds of animals and faces."

"I remember. It was the only time you would be still for more than a couple minutes." I could hear the fond smile in my mother's voice. She missed her great-aunt almost as much as I did. She hadn't had the best family, her parents more concerned with status and how they looked to other people than actually caring about their own flesh and blood, so she'd written them off a long time ago. They were all the same. All except for Sylvia. In a way, the vivacious life-of-the-party had saved us both.

I smiled at the memory of my mom's great-aunt. She had been one of my most favorite people in the whole world, and the closest thing I'd had to a grandmother. My parents divorced when I was little, and my mom chose Hope Valley to start fresh because this was where Sylvia lived. One of the saddest days of my life was the day we lost Aunt Sylvia. She'd been a force of nature. A bright, shining spot in every single day. She'd been instrumental in raising me and teaching me to love myself for who I was. My mom swore up and down that my wild streak came from her, and having known the woman, I didn't doubt that one bit.

As a matter of fact, I was so connected to the woman that I still lived in her house. When we first moved here, she'd insisted my mother and I take the big house while she moved into the small carriage house that had been converted into an apartment. I was nineteen when she passed away at the ripe age of ninety-seven, and Mom and Micah had stayed in the house for a few more years before declaring she was ready for something smaller.

I hadn't wanted to lose the memories we'd formed there, so I bought it from Mom and decided to stay. The elaborate gardens that Sylvia had started decades ago were still thriving, thanks to the green thumb she'd instilled in me. The carriage house apartment was still at the back of the property, as was the tree house Micah built for me when I was little. The walls inside had been repainted, but only because the original bright, vibrate colors had faded, and I wanted to freshen them up. The peacock greens and other jewel tones scattered across the walls might not have been other peoples' style, but it was definitely mine.

I'd loved this house from the time I was four years old, and I couldn't imagine wanting to live anywhere else.

"You know," Mom started, pulling my attention from the lion I'd just found in a big cumulus cloud, "I was talking to Dani the other day. She was telling me that Hardin's divorce is nearly finalized."

I let out a groan and squeezed my eyes closed, knowing exactly where this was going. "God, Mom," I whined, sounding like a bratty teenager. "Don't start on this again. *Please*."

Dani, or Danika Drake, was the owner of Muffin Top and another close, personal friend of my mother's. If she and Mom had been discussing her stepson's recent divorce, it could only mean one thing.

"I don't know what you're talking about," she said innocently. "I'm not starting anything. Just trying to make conversation with my daughter. Is that so bad?"

I rolled my eyes at the sky and sent up a silent prayer for patience. "It is when you think you're being all sneaky while trying to fix me up." I rolled over onto my side, pushing up on my elbow and propping my head on my hand. "The problem with trying to set me up with your friends' kids is that we all basically grew up together, Mom. I know Hardin." He was a great guy, no doubt about that, but there wasn't a chance in hell I would ever date him. My nose scrunched up and my teeth curled. "It would be like trying to date my brother."

She mimicked my position and reached across our mats to brush a tendril of hair off my forehead. "I just want to make sure you aren't lonely, love bug. That's all. You haven't dated anyone in forever."

"I've dated," I cried in offense.

She gave me a look that said she knew I was full of shit, and I had to curl my lips between my teeth to keep from smiling. She knew the truth as well as I did. I hadn't dated anyone in a really long time. It had been two months since my drunken hookup with Connor the night of Rae and Zach's wedding, and even though I kept telling myself I was going to put myself out there again, I flaked. I told myself I would try dating apps, but I hadn't gotten through the registration portion of two I'd downloaded.

If I were being honest with myself—something I'd been trying very hard *not* to be over the past two months— I would admit that I hadn't been able to stop thinking about Connor since creeping out of his room that night.

It didn't help matters much that the damn man hadn't stopped trying to get in touch with me in all that time. I had been so sure he'd push me to the back of his mind and forget all about me, but Lennix had been right. For some reason, the stupid, sexy jerk wasn't giving up. He might have left Hope Valley to hop back on the rodeo circuit, but the phone calls and texts hadn't stopped. Despite every single one of them going unanswered, they hadn't even slowed down.

Some days I deleted his messages without listening or reading. Some days I pretended they didn't exist. And then there were the days I was feeling particularly masochistic. On those days I'd curl up in my bed and listen to every voicemail, read every single text, until that wall I'd built around my heart specifically to keep Connor Bennet out started to wobble.

Those days were dangerous. But so far, I'd held strong.

"I'm perfectly fine being single," I assured my mom as I pushed up to sitting and stretched my back out. I need to focus on work and myself right now. I'm not looking to start anything."

A crease formed between her brows as she studied me with concern. "Are you okay, sweetie?"

My mother's insightfulness never failed to surprise me. Fortunately, I managed to keep my face clear. "I'm totally fine," I assured her, thankful that my voice remained calm and even.

"You sure? Nothing happened?"

I gave my head a shake. "Nope. Not a thing." My stomach lurched again, and this time I wasn't sure if it was the lingering stomach virus or the fact that I was lying to her.

I hated lying to my mom. It wasn't something I'd ever done. I might have been a massive pain in the ass growing up, but I didn't lie. That was a promise I was proud I'd kept all these years, and now I felt like the world's worst daughter.

"Okay." She still sounded skeptical. "But you know you can talk to me about anything, right?"

The cramping in my stomach got gradually worse as my guilt continued to build. "I know, Mom." I offered her a tiny smile, assuring myself that it was a tiny, harmless lie, and the reason I wasn't telling her what went down with Connor was because I didn't want her to worry needlessly. I took another pull from my water bottle, hoping it was dehydration from not being able to keep much down lately that made me feel so lousy. "That's what makes you the best."

Her expression cleared. "Okay, good. I guess I'll get going. I need to get to the flower shop." My mom ran the local flower shop, Divine Flora, that she'd inherited from Sylvia years ago. "But Micah told me to tell you he expects you over for dinner one night this week, and if you even think about cancelling, he's going to show up on your doorstep and physically drag you out. He really misses you."

I let out a laugh, trying to force my stomach to calm the hell down. "I miss him too. You tell me the night and I'll be there. I promise. And give him a hug for me."

She pulled me into a tight hug, the smell of her perfume invading my senses and making my mouth begin to water as I struggled to keep the bile down.

"Love you, sweetheart. I'll talk to you later."

"I love you too." I watched as she rounded the side of

the yard toward the front, keeping my back teeth clamped together as I faked a smile. Then, as soon as she was out of hearing range, I bent over and emptied the limited contents of my stomach into a gardenia bush.

Determination coursed through my blood as my truck cruised over the town limits into Hope Valley. It had been a little over two months since I last saw Ivy, and I was here to put an end to the radio silence once and for all.

When I woke up and found she'd snuck out of my room my first instinct was to be pissed off. Hell, it was still the gut reaction I wanted to jump to more than I was willing to admit, but the hypocrisy of being mad at her for pulling the same shit I had pulled wasn't lost on me. I couldn't blame her for what she'd done. All I could do was try to move us forward.

As badly as I wanted to stay in town after our night together and work things out, I'd had obligations that forced me to leave for a while. I had a couple big ticket rodeos I couldn't miss out on, a photoshoot for an ad from one of my sponsors, and my mother's birthday that I couldn't miss.

This time was different however, because even though I was leaving, I had every intention of coming back as soon as I possibly could. No more avoiding, no more ghosting. We were going to hash this out if it was the last goddamn thing I did. My resolve was strong as I whipped my truck off the asphalt road and onto the gravel lane that took me to Second Hope Lodge. I knew I was about to encounter an uphill battle, but the one thing that kept me going was the fact that two people couldn't have the kind of chemistry we did and ignore it forever. She might still hate me for what I'd done, but I wasn't giving up.

The lodge came into view, and just like last time, my heart was beating staccato against my ribs. Only this time around, it wasn't panic clutching at my chest. Well, not *only* panic, anyway. I would have been lying if I said I wasn't scared sick that she would never be able to forgive me.

I'd taken the past several weeks away to really think about my feelings for Ivy and what I thought I was capable of giving her, and the decision I had finally come to was that I might not deserve her, but I was willing to do everything I possibly could to be the man she would choose anyway. If those months I'd spent on the road after our first night together had taught me anything, it was that a woman like Ivy Young couldn't be worked out of your system. Once she was in, she was there to stay, and if you were lucky enough to experience that, you learned never to let it go.

I wanted her. Christ, I couldn't take a full fucking breath unless she was in the vicinity. My feelings for Ivy made me start to question everything I had with Amber, because, if what I had with the woman I thought I was in love with wasn't even half of what I had with Ivy, had it ever been real?

That particular question had fucked with my head for a while, but I was done letting my fears hold me back. The conversation I'd overheard between her and Lennix the morning of Zach and Rae's wedding had put everything in perspective. I was ready to do some hardcore groveling. If that didn't work, I could always try bribery; I also wasn't above begging.

Whatever it took.

As I parked in the visitor section of the large gravel lot, I realized I probably should have prepared for what I was going to say instead of deciding to wing it, but it was too damn late as I took the steps up the large wrap-around porch at a jog, ignoring the relentless throb in my knee that had only gotten worse, and whipped the door open.

I made my way inside, my destination her office on the

second floor, but I was derailed almost instantly by the sound of Zach saying my name in the form of a question.

My head shot around, my gaze landing on the reception desk where Zach was standing with Rae, Lennix, and their grandmother, Becky. My gaze bounced around among the three of them. Becky looked at me like it was just another day. Rae was too busy looking at something on the computer to give me more than a brief smile. Zach seemed more confused than anything. And Lennix was watching me with wide eyes and her mouth hanging open.

"Hey man." My best friend pushed up from where he'd been leaning against the credenza and moved toward me. "What are you doin' here? I mean, not that it's not good to see you, but I'll admit I'm surprised. You have a rodeo out this way or somethin'?"

There was really no point in beating around the bush, so I decided to just go with the truth. "Uh, no. Actually, I'm here to see Ivy."

His forehead wrinkled as his brows pushed together. "Ivy? Why?"

"*Oh shit*," Lennix muttered under her breath.

I blew a big gust of air past my lips. "Look, I'll explain everything, but I'd really like to talk to her first. Do you know if she's up in her office?"

Lennix pushed away from the reception desk so fast you'd have thought she got bit by a rattlesnake. "I'll go get her for you," she offered. "You just . . . stay down here. I'll be right back."

Before I could get a word out, she turned and bolted up the stairs at an impressive speed—leaving me with her brother who was starting to look at me like I was keeping a secret and he didn't like it one damn bit.

"I starting to get the feelin' I'm missing somethin' here."

"You and me both," Rae said, her scrutinizing gaze no longer on the computer screen but pinned to me.

Well shit.

I could already tell this wasn't going to be any damn fun.

Ivy

I HADN'T KEPT MY PROMISE TO MY MOTHER LAST week to go see the doctor if I didn't start feeling better, but every morning I woke up convinced that this was the day I'd finally feel better. Only, that hadn't happened yet. The exhaustion was so bad I caught myself dozing off at my desk more than once. The nausea refused to let up, making it nearly impossible to keep anything down, and because I wasn't eating or drinking the way I needed, the dizzy spells were getting worse. For the past few weeks my diet consisted of little more than crackers, toast, and ginger ale or 7up. I couldn't remember the last time I felt this lousy; it had gotten beyond ridiculous.

I was contemplating curling up beneath my desk for a quick power nap when the door to my office burst open and Lennix came rushing in with the force of a tornado. She quickly slammed the door behind her, causing me to jump in my seat, and pressed her back against it like she was hiding from somebody . . . or trying to keep somebody out.

"What the hell? You scared the shit out of me."

"Sorry," she said on a pant. "I got a little carried away."

"Why are you out of breath?"

She leaned forward and braced her hands on her knees. "I ran up the stairs. Gah!" She pushed upright and sucked in a huge, dramatic breath. "Cardio, am I right? Do *not* recommend."

I slowly rose to my feet, bracing my hands on the top of my desk when I felt a little unsteady. "Then why the hell did you run up the stairs?"

"Because I had to warn you."

My back went straight, the tightening in my gut having nothing to do with sickness this time. "Warn me about what?" I asked, even though I was afraid I already knew the answer to my own question.

"Connor is downstairs." *And there it is.*

"Shit," I hissed, lifting a shaky hand to my mouth. "Are you serious?"

She nodded, pulling her bottom lip between her teeth. "Yep. Zach and Rae were down there when he came in. Zach asked why he was here, and he blurted out that he was here for you. I'm afraid some secrets are about to come to light down there, and I'm not confident that Zach won't punch the shit out of Connor when he finds out. You're like a little sister to him, you know."

"*Shit!*" I repeated. It was the only word I could think of while my brain was busy trying to process everything Lennix just dumped on me.

She nodded slowly in agreement. "Yeah. Shit is about right. What do you want to do? You want me to get rid of him?"

"Um . . ." I wish that was a viable option, but if Connor was really here, prepared to spill the truth to Zach, I had a feeling he wouldn't be so easily turned away. "I think maybe I have to handle this myself?"

Her brows winged upward. "Was that a question?"

"I don't know!" I cried, throwing my arms up at my sides. "I'm freaking out right now!"

Lennix's hands came up in a placating gesture. "Okay.

It's okay," she soothed. "Everything is going to be fine." She took a sweeping look at me for the first time since barging into my office. "Well, I mean except for the fact you look like death warmed over. Good lord, babe. Are you okay?"

My expression fell flat as I gritted through my clenched teeth, "*Not. Helping.*"

"Sorry. Sorry. Okay, where was I?" She snapped her fingers. "Right. You're fine. It's all gonna be fine. We're going to go downstairs to make sure my brother hasn't committed murder and find out what's going on. I'll be there the whole time, alright? You can do this."

"I can do this," I repeated, hoping if I said it enough times I'd start to believe it. "I can totally do this."

"Yeah, for sure! Now, you ready?"

Hell no, but it looked like I didn't really have much of a choice.

We started out of my office and barely made it to the top of the staircase when we heard raised voices.

Lennix turned to me with big, panicked eyes. "*Shit.*"

I put on a burst of speed, trying to keep up with her, but my body didn't want to cooperate. I barely made it to the first landing when my vision started to get wonky, blurring along the edges.

"Are you fuckin' kidding me?" I heard Zach shout as I rounded the banister.

Rae stepped into her husband. "Okay, I think everyone should just take a breath and try to calm down." She put herself between the two men. Zach looked ready to rip someone's head off while Connor looked resigned to receive a fist to the face.

"Look who I found," Lennix chirped overly brightly as she reached the base of the staircase.

Five sets of eyes swung up my way once I was halfway down the stairs. "Hey," I greeted lamely, lifting my hand in a limp wave as my head began to swim.

"Whoa," Rae breathed out. "Honey, you don't look so good."

Connor rushed my way, climbing up two steps. "Are you okay?"

No, I didn't think I was. "Um . . ." I licked my lips as I reach up to wipe at the sweat suddenly dotting my brow. "Does it seem wobbly in here to anyone else?"

That was the last thing I remembered before my vision went completely black and I fainted in the middle of the staircase.

"This is ridiculous," Ivy grumbled, her mouth pulled down into a pout, her arms folded over her chest insolently. "I told you guys I was fine. There was no need for you to take me to the hospital."

Rae bugged her eyes out at her friend from across the curtained off section of the emergency room we were currently tucked in. "Are you kidding me right now? Ivy, you fainted while standing at the middle of a hard-ass wooden staircase. It's a wonder you didn't kill yourself!"

I hadn't said a word in the past ten minutes as I paced the little room. My emotions were all over the place, tangled around my vocal cords and rendering them useless. I was angry and terrified, and I worried which of those would rush to the surface if I said anything before giving myself enough time to cool down.

I wasn't sure there had ever been a time in my life I'd been more scared than when Ivy's eyes rolled back in her head just a second before she passed the fuck out. If I hadn't already been starting toward her, she would have fallen down those stairs, and Christ only knew how much worse off she would have been.

As it was, I barely caught her in time. But it wasn't just the fact that she nearly took a tumble down a flight of stairs that scared me. It was that once I caught her and got her safely to the bottom, laying her out on the floor, I couldn't get her to wake up.

I didn't know what the hell was wrong with her, and it scared the shit out of me. She was paler than the last time I'd seen her, thinner too. She looked like she'd been sick for a while, and I fucking hated that I hadn't been here to help take care of her.

The reality was that it had only taken a minute for her eyelids to flutter back open, but to me, it felt like a goddamn eternity. Those eight seconds I spent on the back of a bull were nothing compared to the sixty it took for my butterfly to wake up. I didn't breathe for that full minute, my heart on the floor beside her and my throat locked up tight.

Even after she'd regained consciousness, she'd been

sluggish and her words were slurred for a few seconds before she became clearheaded once more. When I announced I was calling an ambulance she'd freaked, argued that she was fine, it was just a little dizzy spell, but I didn't listen. I pulled out my phone, fully prepared to call 911 when she finally relented. She agreed to go to the hospital, but refused to do so in the back of an ambulance.

She started complaining the instant I picked her up and carried her out of the lodge to my truck. My knee screamed with pain at the added weight, but with Ivy's well-being in question, I was able to push it to the back of my mind. The complaining continued the entire drive to the hospital and hadn't stopped since.

"This had gotten ridiculous," Lennix scolded. When I made it clear I was the one who would be taking Ivy to the hospital, Lennix and Rae hadn't hesitated to jump in on the passenger side. I might have argued if I wasn't so focused on getting Ivy taken care of, but now I was glad for the extra company. The three of them could bicker while I tried to loosen the pressure that was currently crushing my chest. "You've been sick for *weeks* now. It never should have come to this. You should have seen a doctor as soon as this started."

The realization that she'd been sick even longer than I suspected and hadn't been taking care of herself made the panic-induced rage I was feeling at that very moment even worse. I wanted to strangle her for being so careless with her health, then wrap her up and hold her in my lap until she was feeling better again.

It struck me in that moment that this was the first time in my life I had ever wanted to take care of another person. Amber hadn't been much of a caregiver while we were together either, so the two of us had an unspoken understanding that whenever the other was sick, we'd just leave them be until they were better. It had worked for us. Or at least I thought it had. But the thought of leaving Ivy alone in her current state damn near bowled me over.

It wasn't going to happen. She could hate me all she wanted, but I wasn't leaving her side until I trusted that she was okay.

"It's just a stomach virus," she continued to argue. "There's nothing to be done. It just needs to run its course."

Rae snorted and rolled her eyes. "Forgive me for wanting to wait to hear what the doctor has to say."

She and I both.

A beat of silence passed through the small enclosure, and I could feel three sets of eyes on me as I continued to pace, feeling like a caged lion.

Finally, Ivy broke it, and what she said managed to piss me off even worse. "You don't have to stick around." When I dragged my gaze to her I saw she was looking directly at me. "I can get a ride home when I'm finished here." She was kicking me out. She was trying to do it politely, sure. But she was attempting to kick me out all the same.

"I'm stayin'," I grunted before resuming my worried pacing.

"Connor, that's really not necessar—"

Her words cut off with a yelp when, one second I was across the room and the next I was hovering over her in that goddamn hospital bed, my fists braced in the flimsy mattress on either side of her as I leaned in so close we were practically nose to nose.

"You took a fuckin' decade off my life. I watched you faint right before my eyes and the only thing I could think was I might not get to you fast enough to keep you from hurtin' yourself. It took a minute for you to wake back up again, butterfly. A fuckin' *minute*, in which time, another seven years was shaved off the end of my life. So now you've cost me seventeen years. The last thing I want to do is yell at you when you're clearly sick, so please, I'm beggin', do us both a favor and let it go, because *I'm. Not. Leavin'.* Understand?"

"What in the fresh hell is happening right now?" Rae whispered loudly from behind me, but I was too busy staring into the eyes of the woman I realized I'd do anything for to pay the other two in the room any mind.

"Let me explain," Lennix started. "This here is an alpha cowboy exerting his dominance. It's something you're more inclined to see in these small towns than in the big city like you're used to."

"Ah, so that's what Zach's doing every time we get into an argument. I thought he was only being a stubborn pain in my ass."

"Oh, he's that too."

My eyes stayed locked on Ivy's big blue gaze as we both ignored the ridiculous conversation behind us. Finally, her throat worked on a thick swallow, her words coming out softly as she said, "O-okay. You can stay."

Goddamn right I could, I thought, but decided it wouldn't be smart to say that out loud.

The silent stare-down was broken a few seconds later when the curtain scraped along the rod as it was pulled open and the doctor walked in. I stayed rooted to the floor right beside Ivy's bed, bracing my feet shoulder-width apart and crossing my arms over my chest as I waited for what he had to say.

"Well, I've gone over your bloodwork and you're going to be fine."

"Told you," she blurted, her snide expression hitting all three of us.

"That isn't to say that what's happening isn't serious. You passed out due to extreme dehydration. Morning sickness is no joke, especially in the early stages of a pregnancy, so I'm going to write you a prescription for a medication that should make it easier for you to keep food and liquids down."

The doctor's voice suddenly sounded like he was beneath water, his words not making a damn bit of sense.

"*Pregnant*?" Rae squeaked.

Lennix threw her hand out in front of her. "Whoa, wait. *What*?"

Ivy's hand went up like she was a middle school student asking the teacher's permission to go to the bathroom or something. "Um, doctor, I'm sorry, but I think you might have the wrong room. I have the stomach flu."

All I could do was stand there like a fucking statue as a record scratched in a loop in my head. *Pregnant. Pregnant. Pregnant* it chirped before that terrible screeching sound. Over and Over.

The man's bushy white brows pulled together in a furrow of confusion as he lifted the chart in his hands. "You're Ivy Young, correct?"

"Yes, but . . . I'm not . . . I can't be . . ." She broke off on a little giggle. "That's not possible."

"I'm sorry." The doctor gave Ivy a gentle look before turning that same one on me. Like we were in this together or something. *What the fuck was happening*? "I thought you knew. Ms. Young, you're eight weeks pregnant."

I wasn't sure how the hell I expected her to react, but it sure as hell wasn't to burst into hysterical laughter that lasted several seconds before she proceeded to pass the fuck out again.

Ivy

AT LEAST I WAS ALREADY SITTING DOWN THE *second time I fainted.*

I was currently in the middle of the most epic freak-out I'd ever experienced in all my twenty-seven years, so I was looking for a silver lining wherever the fuck I could find one.

Pregnant.

I was *pregnant.*

I knew what the word meant, but the more I kept thinking it, the less it made sense. It was like when you repeated a word a bunch of times and it started to sound ridiculous; like fork or spelunking, or taint—the body part, not the verb.

Pregnant.

Nope. Still didn't make a damn bit of sense.

When I came to after my second fainting spell, I was stretched out in the bed with an IV hooked up to the back of my hand, pumping a clear liquid into my body. The doctor was still there, along with a nurse who was in the middle of checking my pulse, but my friends and Connor were gone.

"You're going to be fine, sweetie," the nurse told me with a reassuring smile. "Just a bit of a panic attack. That's all. It's totally normal."

"Really?" I asked dryly. "You have a lot of women come in here thinking they have the stomach flu, find out their pregnant, then pass out on a regular basis?"

She patted my shoulder affectionately. "Happens more often than you'd think."

Well, at least I was in good company.

"I sent your friends out so we could get you hooked up and start getting fluids into you," the doctor explained as he leaned over me and flicked an annoying pen light back and forth between my eyes. "I've administered some anti-nausea meds through your IV and once that bag is empty, you should be able to go home."

I closed my eyes and pulled in a steadying breath, the reality of my situation finally sinking in. "And the baby?" I asked quietly, bringing my hand up to rest on my stomach. "Do you think the baby is okay?"

He smiled and patted my hand. "Your baby is just fine.

However, given how intense your morning sickness has been, I'd suggest scheduling an appointment with your obstetrician as soon as possible, but you have nothing to worry about. Once you're eating and drinking normally, you'll be shocked at how quickly you'll return to normal."

I dropped my head back on the paper-thin pillow and looked up at the ceiling tiles. After today, I wasn't sure what normal looked like. All I knew was that my life had irrevocably changed forever.

Anxiety made it impossible for me to sit still. The waiting room of the emergency room was only half full and surprisingly silent, making the click of my boot heel on the cold, hard floor that much louder as my knee jiggled uncontrollably.

I let out a huff as I recalled Ivy going down for the second time, falling backward onto the bed after her laughing fit, and being kicked out of the room by the doctor. I'd tried refusing at first, but he said I could either leave on my own and sit in the waiting room or be escorted out by security. The old man might have looked like Santa's less jolly brother, but when he hit me with a cold, steely look that said he wasn't fucking around, he reminded me more of Clint Eastwood holding a rifle on the kids who dared to step on his lawn.

I let Lennix and Rae guide me from the curtained space without issue, knowing it was the only way to stay close to Ivy . . . and my child she was carrying.

Christ! She was pregnant with *my* child. And I didn't have the first fucking clue how to feel about it.

Leaning forward, I braced my elbows on my knees and clasped my hands together in front of my mouth as I tried to wrap my head around everything. One moment I was pissed off that she hadn't been taking care of herself and worried that it was something worse than a stomach virus, and the next I was finding out I was going to be a father.

A father!

I wasn't against having kids or anything. In fact, there had been a point in my life where I believed I'd have at least one. But I thought that ship had sailed. After Amber and I split and I told myself I was never going down that road again, I just figured that meant kids weren't in the cards.

My knee picked up the pace as Rae and Lennix's eyes bored into the side of my face, and one quick glance told me they were both aware I was losing my shit and felt bad for me.

"Jesus," I grunted, pushing to my feet and scrubbing my clammy palms against my jeans as I began to pace. "How long is this doctor gonna take?"

"Connor, I'm sure she's fine," Rae offered in a soothing voice.

A shot her a quick look before rubbing a hand over my face. "Then why'd he kick us out when she went down, huh?"

"Uh . . . because you started freaking out, and he couldn't deal with your shit and check on her at the same time," Lennix said like the answer was obvious. And, damn it, she might have been right. I hadn't exactly been in the best frame of mind.

"Do you think . . .?" A sudden ache in my chest had me rubbing at my sternum. "Do you think there's something wrong with the baby?"

Lennix stood up and walked over to me, placing a comforting hand on my forearm. "I'm sure everything is perfectly fine. You heard what he said. She's super dehydrated. I'm sure they'll take care of her and she'll be feeling better in no time."

I blew a slow stream of air past my pursed lips and nodded. "Yeah. Okay." I nodded, grabbing onto what she said and treating it as fact. "You're right. She'll be fine. Everything will be fine."

The doors to the emergency bays swung open and the doctor who'd been treating Ivy came out. I immediately shot in his direction. "Is she okay? Has she woken up yet? Are you sure it's not more than dehydration?"

He held up his hands to halt my frantic line of questioning. "Ms. Young is perfectly fine," he answered with certainty. "I have an IV hooked up to her as we speak, giving her fluids her body has needed. Dehydration on her level can lead to dizzy spells, and it's not uncommon for the person to faint since their body is diverting all the necessary nutrition to the baby. That, coupled with stress, set off a panic attack. Her body needed a little break. She and the baby are fine. In fact, as soon as the IV bag is empty, I feel confident releasing her."

The man's eyes darted between the three of us gathered around him. "I assume there is someone who can look after her at home?"

"Yes." I blurted the word out before he'd finished his sentence, making it clear that I would be the one looking after Ivy, no one else. "I will. I'll take care of her."

"Great. I'll get started on the discharge paperwork. I'll also include a prescription for anti-nausea medication that is safe for both mother and baby, as well as things that can be done to alleviate it naturally. It's best to stick with bland foods for a few days until we're certain she can keep it down. A BRAT diet would be best. And I've also instructed her to make an appointment with an obstetrician at her earliest convenience. In the meantime, she needs plenty of rest."

I was nodding so much by the time he finished rattling off his instructions, I felt like a bobble head. I didn't have the first clue what the hell a BRAT diet was, but I was sure I could figure it out. "BRAT. Obstetrician. Got it."

I didn't have it. Not at all. I felt seconds away from a panic attack myself, but I knew I needed to suck it the hell up and take care of this for her. She'd been dealing with everything alone for the past several weeks, now it was time for me to step up and carry the weight so she could get better.

I could do this. I *had* to do this.

"She's resting right now, so you can come on back and sit with her while she finishes with her IV fluids."

I took a step, intent on following after the doctor, when I felt a tug on my arm. I stopped and looked back over my shoulder at Rae and Lennix.

"We're going to let you handle this," Rae informed me with a resolute nod. "I think there's a lot the two of you need to talk about, and it's probably best if you guys don't have an audience."

I gave her a small chin dip. "Appreciate that. You guys have a ride home?"

One corner of Lennix's mouth hooked up. "Zach's on his way to pick us up. Don't worry. We'll keep him from storming in here and kicking your ass."

"You aren't—"

Rae elbowed Lennix in the ribs and shook her head.

"Don't worry. We aren't going to tell anyone. This isn't our news to share. It needs to come from you guys."

I gave them one last nod then spun around and booked it through the double doors, needing to be close to Ivy.

HER COLOR HAD ALREADY IMPROVED AFTER ONE bag of IV fluids. When I'd returned to her room earlier, I could tell she was still feeling as shellshocked as I was, so neither of us spoke as we waited for the bag to drain.

That had been an hour ago. She'd been discharged from the hospital and I'd driven her back home in complete silence. I understood she had a lot to process. Hell, we both did. But the silence was starting to drive me out of my goddamn mind. I needed to know what she was thinking. How she was feeling. If she knew what she wanted to do, because I felt like I couldn't move, couldn't take that first step, until I knew what direction she wanted to go in.

I made the drive from the hospital to her house with a whole new awareness. I didn't think I'd been this cautious of a driver since I was sixteen and wanted to prove to my folks that I was a responsible driver so they'd get me my own car. I now knew the meaning of the phrase, precious cargo, because I was petrified of doing something that could possibly hurt Ivy or the baby she was carrying. There was no way in hell I would put either of them at risk, so I was slow with the gas pedal and eased to a roll before braking so I didn't jerk her around and cause the seatbelt to cut into her middle. *Was that even a thing?*

I didn't know, but I wasn't taking any risks. I didn't miss the way her eyes kept cutting over to the speedometer, but I refused to go any faster than I was going, which happened to be about five miles below the speed limit.

When we finally pulled up outside her house, I felt like I was coming out of my skin.

"Thanks for the ride," she muttered as she grabbed the door handle.

"No problem," I replied as I shifted into park and push the ignition button, killing the engine.

Her brows rose high as she stared at me. "What are you doing?"

I felt my forehead pinch with confusion as I looked across the cab at her. "I'm coming around so I can help you down."

The frustrated huff she let out would have probably been cute if I didn't feel like we'd both been put through the wringer. "That's really not necessary, Connor. I'm not an invalid. I'm just p-pregnant." She stuttered out the last word.

"I'm aware, butterfly. But you've also passed out twice today and had to have a hospital administer fluids because you weren't able to do it yourself."

Her eyelids narrowed into a glare, and I couldn't help but wonder if there was something wrong with me, because seeing that fire return to her eyes for the first time today sent a wave of relief through me and turned me on at the same damn time. "I'm more than capable of taking care of myself. You don't need to stick around. I'm fine on my own."

I hit the locking button before she could throw the door open, keeping her from escaping. "Ivy, I'm not leavin'. You heard what the doctor told you. You shouldn't be alone right now. I'm stayin' to make sure you're all right."

The fight drained out of her as quickly as it appeared. One moment she was sitting across from me, glaring daggers, and the next she was heaving out a sigh so heavy it made her shoulders droop and massaging her temples. I wasn't sure I'd ever seen her look so tired.

"Connor, I really can't do this right now, okay? I'm exhausted and . . . stressed, and I only want to lie down and go to sleep for the next two days. I appreciate you wanting to look after me, but I need some space right now, okay? I need some time to think."

I swallowed to try and ease the desert-like conditions in my throat. I wanted to push, to ask her what she needed to think about. Did she need to think about us? About me? About whether or not she wanted to keep the baby? I wanted to crack her head open and find out what was going on inside. But this hill I had to climb to get back to her was already steep enough, and the events of today only made it more treacherous.

"Okay," I finally relented on a whisper, every single molecule in my body rebelling at the thought of leaving her alone. "I get it. But can you just promise me one thing?"

"What's that?"

"Once you're feeling better, promise you'll talk to me? You aren't alone in this, Ivy." I wanted so badly to reach across the center console and touch her; skim my knuckles over her cheek or brush her hair back. Anything to feel connected. "We're in this together, okay? Just . . . promise you won't cut me out. Not with this."

She sniffled, her blue eyes growing glassy as she gave me a single nod. Then she climbed out of my truck.

I gave myself a few moments to collect my thoughts before throwing the driver side door open and climbing out just to climb back into the back seat. I was a pro when it came to sleeping in my truck. Lord knows I'd done it enough while traveling from rodeo to rodeo—I even kept a pillow and blanket back there to make things more comfortable. I stretched out as best I could and shifted around to make myself more comfortable.

I promised her I would give her some space, but I also said I'd look after her, and if I had to do that by sleeping in my truck outside her house, so be it. I was taking care of that woman if it was the last thing I did.

Chapter Seventeen

IVY

I didn't sleep for almost two days, but it was damn close.

When I finally did wake up, so much time had passed that I wasn't sure what time it was. Or even what day it was. The bone-deep exhaustion that had been clinging to me like a needy koala for weeks had finally lightened up, and once I'd showered, going through my whole skin and haircare routine, and put on fresh clothes, I felt like a brand-new person.

I'd decided to call off work for another day to make sure I didn't backslide, and spent that time curled up on my couch in front of the television and talking to Rae and Lennix to assure them I really was all right.

"So he's still there?"

At Rae's question I crunched into a piece of

buttered toast as I stood at the window that overlooked my driveway. Apparently, while I'd been catatonic, Connor had taken it upon himself to camp out in my driveway—his compromise on giving me space—so he wasn't in my face, but close enough to help if I needed it.

"Yep." I crunched the bite and swallowed it down as I stared at the shadowy figure curled up in the back seat of Connor's truck. How a man his size could sleep comfortably in such a tiny space was beyond me. "I feel a little bad," I admitted, my hand drifting down to rest on my stomach for the millionth time that day. It was like now that I knew there was a teeny tiny living thing inside there, I couldn't stop touching it. "He has to be miserable, right? Squeezed in there like that?"

"If he didn't need a chiropractic adjustment before, I'm sure he needs one now," Rae said, making me feel even worse for leaving him out there all this time instead of letting him in. I would have been lying if I said I hadn't melted just a little when I found out he'd been sleeping in my driveway, refusing to leave in case I needed him. It was that side of him that he'd shown me when we were first getting to know each other. The side that caused me to start falling for him. With how things had ended, it had been easy to forget all the good things I learned about him over those months. Now I was starting to remember, and it made my resolve to keep him out of my life for good that much weaker.

I'd taken the time I'd been awake to really think about this pregnancy and what it meant for my life, and while there was a part of me that was terrified of what was to come, there was also a larger part that was excited.

Sure, the path to having my own family had been a lot different when I pictured it in my head, but the outcome was still the same. I was going to have a baby. And the more I reminded myself of that, the more connected I felt to the little bean growing inside of me.

Heaving out a breath, I let go the wooden blinds and let them fall back into place before stepping away from the window. "You're right. I'll let you go. It's probably time I talk to him anyway. He's been out there for two days."

"Okay, sweetie. Call me if you need anything. I'm here for you. We all are."

I wasn't sure if it was the stress from the past couple days or the pregnancy hormones that suddenly had me feeling weepy. "Thanks, honey. Love you."

"Love you back."

I disconnected the call and pulled in a fortifying breath, trying to summon the courage to talk to Connor. I made him that promise a couple days earlier, and I intended to keep it. The sun had already started to dip behind the mountains along the horizon, casting the sky in beautiful shades of purple that started off as a soft lavender before deepening into indigo the lower it got. My slippers scuffed along the concrete of my driveway as I trudged out my back door to Connor's truck, pulling my cardigan tighter around me to ward off the chill in the air that came with the darkening sky.

Through his tinted windows I could see his large form folded up in the back seat in a position that looked uncomfortable. His legs were wedged between the two front seats and stretching almost all the way to the dash. One arm was thrown over his eyes, and the other was flopped off the bench seat beneath him and resting on the floor. He looked miserable, and I felt like an asshole.

When I knocked on the glass to get his attention, his whole body jolted. He bolted upright, smacking his head on the roof of the cab at the same time his elbow flew back and slammed into the window. "Motherfucking fucker! Shit ass goat fucker!" he shouted, rubbing at his sore appendages.

"Sorry! Sorry," I squeaked holding my hands up and jumping back from the door just as he flung it open. "I'm sorry, I didn't mean to scare you."

He finagled himself out of the backseat, still rubbing at his head as he gave me a squinty-eyed look. "Are you . . . *laughing*?"

I curled my lips between my teeth and bit down to keep from smiling as I gave my head a shake.

He rubbed at his eyes and let out a jaw-cracking yawn as he stretched himself out. "Everything okay? Do you need me to take you back to the hospital?"

"No, no. Everything's fine," I assured him, appreciating his concern. "I was, um . . ." I tugged at the collar of my T-shirt and cleared my throat. "I was wondering if you wanted to come inside. To talk," I added quickly so he wouldn't get the wrong idea. "I promised that when I was ready, I'd talk to you, and, well, I'm ready if you are."

His Adam's apple bobbed on a swallow. "Yeah. Yeah, sure. I'm ready. If you're ready I'm totally ready."

The corner of my mouth ticked up in a little grin, the nervous rambling making him a little more endearing to me.

It was like a switch flipped the moment Connor stepped across the threshold and into my house. I was suddenly nervous to share my space with him. He'd only been here one other time, and that visit hadn't exactly ended well.

He was so damn big that every room he entered felt smaller in his presence. I couldn't stop wondering what he thought of the eclectic artwork or the old velvet mismatched furniture in a wide array of bright colors.

I fidgeted in place, twisting my fingers together in front of me as he took in Aunt Sylvia's old macrame designs on the walls or the wild paint choices. Last time we'd been a little too busy trying to kiss each other's faces off so I didn't think he'd been paying much attention to his surroundings.

"Didn't notice how colorful it was in here before," he said softly as he turned in a circle, taking in what he could see from the living room area. "I love it."

My brows pinched in surprise. "You do?"

"Of course." He grinned at me then, wide enough to make those dimples of his pop. "It's you. Wild and bright and fun. It matches your personality perfectly."

My cheeks infused with heat as I lowered my face. "Thanks," I whispered.

He took a step closer, closing enough of the distance between us that I could smell his woodsy, leathery scent. I'd always loved how he smelled. It was rugged and manly and sexy. And it was doing crazy things to my insides. "How are you feeling?"

"I'm okay, actually. A lot better. That medicine the doctor gave me really worked wonders."

"I'm glad to hear that." A shiver ran through me at his gentle tone, and when he reached up to tuck a lock of hair behind my ear, his rough fingers scraping lightly at the sensitive skin on my neck, my whole body broke out in goosebumps.

I took a quick step back, knowing I needed to put distance between us, mainly because of how badly I wanted to lean into his touch. "Um . . . do you want something to drink? I have water, iced tea, soda . . . or I got a new ale from Lennix that they just introduced at the Tap Room. It's really good." My features pulled into a slight pout. "I won't be able to drink it now so you might as well finish it off."

Damn, and I'd really been looking forward to enjoying that beer too.

His smile stretched wider and I told myself that the fluttering sensation in my tummy was pregnancy related; I was full of shit. "Water is fine."

"Great," I chirped, my nerves making my voice higher than I'd intended. "Just, uh . . . take a load off, I guess. I'll be right back."

I whipped around and power-walked into the kitchen like my ass was on fire. "Good lord, get your shit together," I scolded myself on a whisper before whipping the refrigerator open and stuffing my face inside to cool my burning skin.

It wasn't like the guy was a stranger, yet for some reason I was acting like a freaking virgin on prom night. Which was laughable, given that the predicament we were in was proof of just how far from a virgin I actually was.

Filling a glass from the tap, I headed back into the

living room, determined to get this over with. It was a serious talk that needed to be had, and I figured the best way to handle it was to just get it over with.

"Here you go." I handed him the glass and moved over to the deep blue wingback chair across from the couch where Connor was sitting, snuggling into the plush cushion and pulling my feet up to tuck beneath me. I waited as he drank, watching how his throat worked as he swallowed down the water before diving right in.

"So, I've given this a lot of thought, and I decided I want to keep the baby."

His shoulders slumped on a sigh. "I'm really glad," he said with relief, and I realized then that I'd been worried he might be disappointed with my decision. Hearing that he was happy about it eased a lot of the tension that had my shoulders bunched up around my ears.

I hugged my knees tighter to my chest. "I want you to know that I don't expect anything from you. You can be as involved as you want to be, and if you decide this isn't something you want, I'm totally okay with that. I can raise this baby on my own. I don't want you to think you're being pressured into anything. This was a shock for both of us, and I get that you might need more time to figure out what you want to do. I know how impor-tant your job is for you, and I don't want you to think I expect you to give anything up so you can move here and help out. I'm good. I'm fine, really. I can do this by myself."

I didn't realize that I'd been rambling, pouring every sentence out without taking a single breath, until I finished on a heavy exhale, expelling the air that had been trapped in my lungs.

I clamped my mouth shut and waited for his response. I wasn't sure what I'd been expecting, but it sure hadn't been for him to shoot off the couch with a barked, "What the fuck?"

My chin jerked back, my eyes widening. "I—what?"

Connor's face was growing redder by the second. "What. The. *Fuck*?" he repeated in a booming voice that made me jump.

"I-I don't understand."

He reached up and raked his fingers through his hair before rubbing at the back of my neck. "Christ, I knew you hated me, but I didn't realize your opinion of me was that low. You really think I'd abandon my responsibilities? That I'd bail on my own fucking child?"

"I—" I shook my head, unsure of what to say in light of his anger. "I'm sorry. I didn't think . . ."

"You might think I'm a piece of shit, but I'm going to be a part of this baby's life."

I wasn't sure I could have felt any lower than I did in that very moment. "I don't think that," I said on a whisper, my eyes burning with tears I was frantically trying to blink away.

"Could have fooled me."

He turned on his boot and started out of the living room, and without giving it a single thought, I shot out of the chair and followed after him. "Where are you going?"

He paused with the front door open, his head falling forward as he massaged the back of his neck. I hated the defeated slump of his shoulders, and I hated that it was my fault. "I'm going for a drive. I need some air."

"But . . ." I bit down on the inside of my cheek to stop myself from crying. I wasn't a big crier, but this was the third time in less than thirty minutes that the desire to bawl had come over me. If this was an indicator of what the next several months were going to be like I was *not* looking forward to it. "I thought we were going to talk."

"We will," he said, his tone void of any emotion. "But right now I'm the one that needs a little space."

With that, he pulled the door closed behind him, leaving me feeling like the worst person in the world.

God, I was such a prick.

I knew the instant I drove away from Ivy's house I was making a mistake, but after she told me she had no problem raising the baby—*my* baby—without me, how she didn't expect anything from me, not even the most basic fucking support, I hadn't been able to pull in a full breath. I had to get out of there before I did or said something I would have ended up regretting, all because she'd taken my pride and stuffed it into a goddamn woodchipper.

I had every intention of going back. I had to. There was too much on the line, too much at stake for me to take off again. I needed to get my head together first. So I went to the only place where I knew I'd be able to do that.

I lost track of time, the dark sky outside the barn

giving nothing away as to how late it was, while I worked my way through all the stalls, mucking each and every one by myself and tossing down new straw until the muscles in my back and arms felt like they were on fire.

Once I cleaned every stall, I pushed a cart of hay along the alleyway, dropping a flake in each horse's feeding bucket. The familiar smells of the big animals and the hay and earth—hell, even the manure—helped to soothe the dull throb in the center of my chest, but it didn't get rid of it completely.

That was how Zach found me, sweat drenching through my shirt and slicking back my hair as I worked like a man possessed, just me and the companionable silence of the animals around me. "Jesus, man. How long have you been out here?"

I braced one hand on my hip and wiped at the sweat slicked across my forehead with the back of my wrist. "I'm not sure," I answered honestly. "What time is it?"

His eyes widened, his brows inching toward his hairline. "Just after two in the mornin'." His answer took me aback. I hadn't realized how long I'd been lost in my own head until then. Now that he mentioned it, I could see the puffiness of his eyes and his disheveled hair, telling me he'd been asleep until very recently.

"Sorry, man. I needed to clear my head and this was the only place I felt like I could do that."

He moved closer. The anger that had been etched into the planes of his face the last time I saw him were gone, replaced with concern. "It's all good." The last time we spoke, he'd been ready to knock my teeth out for screwing around with Ivy, so it surprised me when he walked over and clapped a hand on my shoulder. "I know what you need. Come with me."

I followed him through the barn and down a long hallway at the back that led to Rae's office. He waved me to the couch pushed up against the back wall and headed for the mini fridge in the corner. He opened it and pulled out two beers, uncapping both and handing one to me before taking a drink from his own bottle.

I took the bottle, clutching it in my hands and letting the cold seep into my palms. "How'd you know I was here?"

He lowered his beer bottle and swallowed. "Ivy called Rae. She knew it was late but said the two of you got into a fight and you left her place upset. She was really worried."

"Fuck," I hissed, leaning forward and scrubbing at the top of my head. "I'm such a dick."

"Way she explained it, she made it sound like she had an equal part in whatever went down. You're an asshole, but I'm sure it's not anything you can't fix." He shot me a wink to let me know he was teasing. "Sometimes the best thing to do during a fight is get a little space in order to gain perspective. She wasn't sure where you would have gone, only that you said you needed to go for a drive. I made an educated guess and decided to check out here. It's all good. I shot a text to the girls to let them know I found you."

"So you aren't still pissed at me?" I asked before I took a swig of beer. The icy cold liquid felt refreshing as it slid down my parched throat.

He barked out a laugh. "Oh, no. I'm still pissed." One corner of his mouth hooked up in a smirk. "But seein' you like this . . ." He waved a hand in front of me. "I feel like I'd be kickin' a man when he's already down."

I snorted out a laugh. "Thanks a lot, shithead."

He grabbed the back of the chair in front of Rae's desk and spun it around so it was facing me before plopping down in it and kicking his legs out straight in front of him, crossing one booted ankle over the other. "So, you want to tell me what's got you so worked up that you're in my barn in the middle of the night scrubbin' out horse stalls so well you can practically eat off the floors? Not that I'm complainin'. You saved my ass at least half a day's work."

I braced my forearms on my knees with a weary sigh, my shoulders feeling heavy as the weight of everything sank down on top of me. "Ivy's pregnant."

Zach proceeded to choke on the drink he'd taken, spitting beer across Rae's office and hacking up a lung. "What?" he croaked, his eyes watering.

I lifted my head and met his gaze. "She's pregnant. It wasn't a stomach virus. It was a baby."

He collapsed back in his chair, his expression properly gobsmacked. "Fuckin' hell. I knew you'd been crashin' outside her house the past couple days, but I thought you were just worried 'cause she's been sick. I didn't realize— Jesus."

"Yep." I popped the P loudly and took another healthy pull from my bottle.

"And I assume it's yours?"

I nodded. That was a question I hadn't needed to ask. I knew the truth of that in my bones just like I knew the type of person Ivy was, and there wasn't a doubt in my mind that the baby she was carrying was mine.

"And that's why you're here? Because you're freaking out."

I stared down at the amber glass in my hands as I picked at the label with my thumbnail. "Yeah, but not how you're thinkin'." I sat back, shaking my head and rubbing absent-mindedly at my messed-up knee. "Don't get me wrong, I'm fuckin' terrified. I mean, what the hell do I know about raisin' a baby? One moment my life is going in this direction, and the next I'm suddenly going to be responsible for keeping this tiny human being alive." I shook my head at the irony of it all. "But when I'm not scared out of my mind, I'm actually a little excited. And if this had to happen with anyone, I'm glad it's with her."

I couldn't imagine doing this with anyone else, of *wanting* it with anyone else. When she told me earlier that she wanted to keep the baby, I hadn't expected the level of relief I felt. Because the fact was, I wanted it too. And I wanted it with Ivy.

"So . . . what's the problem?"

"The problem is I'm not so sure she feels the same way about me." Just remembering back to everything she said was like having a knife shoved into my gut and the blade twisted violently. "Today was the first time she's been ready to talk about this since we found out, and the first goddamn thing she said to me was that she could raise this baby on her own. She said she didn't expect anything from me and was fine doing all this without me."

"Christ," he breathed, hissing out a breath between his teeth. "That's really rough, man. I'm sorry."

"Thanks." I roughed my palm over the stubble on my jaw that had grown thicker the past couple days. When you were basically living out of your truck, there wasn't really a proper place to shave. Since I'd been camped out in her driveway, not wanting to venture too far in case she needed something, I'd been living off fast food, to-go coffee, and functioning on shitty sleep—when I managed to doze off, that was. Most of the time I just lay awake, trying to think of ways to make this right for Ivy.

"I don't know what the fuck to do, man. I don't know how to make her trust me. Or that I even deserve it." Every time I thought of how badly I'd made a mess of everything, it felt like another weight was added to my chest. "I really fucked things up."

"Look, an accidental pregnancy isn't the end of the world."

"No. Not that. I . . ." I had a feeling Zach wouldn't care about kicking a man when he was down after I told him the full story of what happened between Ivy and me, but I needed to put it out there. It felt like saying it out loud to someone else might be the first step to fix it.

"The night of your wedding wasn't the first time Ivy and I slept together," I started. Then I told him about the months I'd spent getting to know her, getting to *like* her. The months where I inevitably fell for the woman despite denying it to myself. Then I confessed what I did after I took her to bed. By the time I finished the muscle in Zach's jaw was so damn tight I was sure he'd cracked at least one tooth.

"*Fuck*," he barked out after a few seconds of silence. "Brother, you have no idea how badly I want to punch you in the goddamn face right now."

I arched a brow in his direction. "You think it would

make you feel better?" I wasn't a fan of getting hit—that had never been a kink of mine—but I had a strange feeling having him punch me might make me feel better as well. Kind of like a penance, or act of contrition. "If you think it'll help, go for—*goddamn it*!"

My head snapped back with the force of his jab. Stars burst before my eyes and blood instantly gushed from my nose. "*Fuck*, that hurt."

Zach straightened up, shaking out his hand as I pinched the bridge of my nose and tilted my head back. "Feel better?"

"I do, actually." He rounded the desk and searched around for a second before returning with a box of tissues, tossing it in my lap before resuming his seat. "And don't be such a baby. I pulled that punch so I wouldn't break your nose. You'll be just fine."

I couldn't stop the chuckle that worked its way up my throat. Shaking my head, I stuffed the tissue into my nostril to staunch the bleeding. With one raised brow, I asked, "We good now?"

He nodded. "We're good. So what are you gonna do about all this shit with Ivy?"

"Christ, I don't know," I grunted. "If it was as easy as letting her punch me in the face to fix this, I'd gladly take another hit, but something tells me that won't be nearly enough." I tossed the bloody tissue into the trash basket beside the couch and lifted the beer bottle to my face, pressing the cold glass against my skin to help with the swelling. "What do you think I should do?"

He drank his beer, mulling my question over. "Well, I guess you can start by asking yourself what it is *you* want."

A few months back, the answer to that question wouldn't have been that easy. My head was too twisted see what I'd had right in front of me. I let the shit with Amber and Dusty and that fuckface Vance fuck with me for too damn long. Now that I'd managed to pull my head out of my ass, the answer was as simple as breathing.

"Her," I said, the answer immediate and resolute. "I want her." And the baby we'd made together without even realizing.

He shrugged casually, saying, "Then you fight for her, brother."

"You make it sound so easy," I grumbled around the mouth of my beer bottle.

"Oh, it's not gonna be easy at all." He chuckled, giving his head a shake. "It'll be hard as hell. But if you're serious about her, it's what you have to do. You fight, and you don't stop fighting. Not for a single second. You do everything it takes, pull out all the stops to prove she can trust you, to make her believe you're in to the very end."

I could do that. I could fight. If I was stubborn enough to hold on to a pissed-off bull dead set on stomping me to death night after night, I could be stubborn enough to see this through.

"You really think that'll work?"

"I don't have a fuckin' clue whether or not it'll work." He let out a laugh. "That's her call, man. But if it's any consolation, I'll be rooting for you. Silently, of course, and from a distance. Just in case it *doesn't* work and she decides to keep hating you. Publicly, I'll be on her side. It's safer that way. Can't let Rae get wind that I don't have her girl's back, you understand."

Fuckin' hell.

Chapter Nineteen

IVY

I sat in my office chair, staring out at the view beyond the windows, lost in thought as my fingers skimmed my stomach. I couldn't seem to stop touching it, like my fingertips or the palm of my hand made the connection with the little thing growing inside me that much stronger. If I was like this now, where there was nothing at all to see, I could only imagine what I'd be like once I started showing.

On a deep breath, I looked away from the glass and down at my flat belly, wondering how it was even possible to love something with your whole heart that you couldn't feel or see or touch. The only reason I knew it existed—aside from the morning sickness that was still sticking around, though much more manageable now—was because a doctor told me so. Yet I knew I couldn't possibly love anything or anyone as much as I loved it.

And because of that love, I knew I had to make things right between me and this little chickpea's father. There were a million different ways to have a family. It wasn't required that Connor and I be together in order to raise this baby in a happy, healthy home. There was no reason we couldn't co-parent successfully, but that wouldn't happen as long as we hated each other. At the very least, our chickpea deserved two parents who got along.

When he'd driven away last night, I'd spent hours pacing my house, chewing on my thumbnail and worrying my cuticles until I made a mess of them. My anxiety that something bad might happen grew and grew until I couldn't take it anymore and ended up calling Rae in the middle of the night.

It wasn't until I knew he was safe on the ranch and Zach was with him that I'd been able to relax. He'd looked so defeated, and I hated the thought of him being alone with those feelings. Knowing he had a friend in his corner put me at ease, but sleep had been impossible. I'd tossed and turned all night, picturing the sadness lurking in his eyes at what I said. I hadn't meant to hurt him, I didn't want him to think I intended to trap him, or that I expected he give up the life he'd worked for because one of the stupid condoms decided not to do its job. I didn't want him to think he had to put a ring on my finger in order to make things right. But I made a mess out of the whole thing, and instead of putting his mind at ease, I'd insulted him.

I hated that he left thinking I had such a low opinion of him. Despite everything, I knew he was a good person, a good man. He did some shitty things, sure. But who hadn't? I wasn't really one to judge on that front. The truth was, I knew down to my soul I could trust Connor to be a good father to our child.

Rising from the chair, I walked over to the huge wall of glass and looked at the ranch below. The barn was too far away for me to see from here, and I wasn't sure he was there, but that didn't stop me from trying to see if I could somehow spot him from the safety of my perch.

"I have it on good authority that he's down at the pen helping Zach with a couple new fillies that came in yesterday."

I turned to look over my shoulder, spotting Rae standing in the doorway of my office, her arms crossed over her chest and her shoulder propped on the doorframe. She was dressed in her version of business attire: a pair of jeans that looked like they might have been an offshoot of her previous life in the city, a pair of boots, and a pretty floral top that was the perfect combination of casual and smart. Since she managed ranching operations and did that out of an office tucked into the barn, she was able to dress more casually than I was.

There wasn't a dress code at the lodge, per se, but I didn't want our guests to think this was some backwoods, hick operation, so today I was wearing a pair of wide-leg black slacks, a silky cream blouse, and black patent leather pumps with four-inch heels.

I shot a smile in her direction. I didn't bother lying and telling her I wasn't searching for Connor. We both knew the truth. "And that good authority would be you, right? Since you just came from that way?"

She pushed off the door frame and lifted her shoulder in a shrug. "Maybe. I figured the two of you might want to talk. Without an argument breaking out this time."

She'd figured right. I'd spent the first half of the day trying to summon the courage to seek him out, and there was no point in delaying it any longer.

"Thanks, Rae."

She turned, offering a smile over her shoulder. "You can thank me by talking to him. It's not about you two anymore. You have someone else to consider."

She disappeared down the hallway, leaving me alone to consider the wisdom of her words, and in less than a minute, I was following the same path she'd taken, heading out the back of the lodge to the shed where we kept the UTVs for staff members who needed to get from one place on the ranch to another without climbing onto a horse.

I didn't know if the two of them were in cahoots, or what, but Zach was standing outside the barn when I pulled up and parked the UTV beside the line of ranch trucks the cowboys and ranch hands used.

"Hey," I greeted with a wave as he pulled off his work gloves and tucked them into the back pocket of his jeans.

"Hey, honey." He gave a long, scrutinizing look. "You look a lot better than the last time I saw you."

"Thanks." I offered a grin. "I feel better."

He crossed his arms over his chest, his lips curving upward. "I heard congratulations are in order."

I lifted my hand unconsciously and placed it on my belly. "Uh, yeah. It's still a little bit of a shock. But it's good news."

"For the both of you." His eyes held mine intently. "He's a good man, sweetheart."

"I know," I replied instantly. "I know, Zach. Things are just . . . complicated."

"I get that." He reached out and gave my forearm an affectionate squeeze. "But I have no doubt the two of you can work this out together. Just have patience with one another, yeah?"

The lump in my throat made my voice come out raspier than normal. "Yeah, Zach. We'll do that."

He gave me a nod, leaning in to place a brotherly kiss to my cheek before moving past me. I headed through the barn, stopping for a moment at Gretel's enclosure to say hi and give her a little loving before moving on to the pen where they trained the new horses.

Connor stood in the center of the pen beside the big black animal, and the sight of him shirtless in a pair of faded jeans and dusty boots caused my mouth to dry right up. The jeans hugged his firm, round ass and thick thighs. His skin was a beautiful golden tan and stretched over defined muscles that flexed and rolled as he stroked a hand along the horse's nose in a soothing gesture.

I was already well aware of the man's physique, but something about seeing him like this, on display, his body shimmering with sweat from a hard day's work, made all the moisture in my body travel south. My panties were damp and my nipples hard just from looking at him. It was like I was in a trance. I didn't realize I was staring until his voice broke through.

"If you want me to flex for you, butterfly, all you have to do is say so. I'm more than happy to put on a show."

My cheeks heated instantly, and I pulled my bottom lip between my teeth to keep my smile at bay. "Who said anything about wanting a show?"

He glanced at me over his shoulder, his smirk making

his dimples pop. "Figured it was what you wanted with how hard you were starin'."

"I wasn't staring." His cheeky grin told me he knew I was full of shit. I rolled my eyes on a huff and gave in. "Oh, all right. I was staring. But come on, you know what you look like."

The chuckle he let loose worked wonders in easing the tension that had been wrapped around my muscles since he drove away the night before. He gave the horse a loving pat on its side before sauntering toward me. I figured since I'd been caught once, might as well make the most of it, and ogled the living shit out of him as he drew closer. I knew from the stories he told me that his body wasn't honed in a gym, but on the back of a bull. He exercised occasionally to stay in shape, but his firm pecs and the ridges formed across his abdomen were mostly from riding.

He stopped across the railing from me and braced his forearms on the top rung of the metal panel that separated us, making his biceps pop. "You get your fill or you want me to go back and take that walk again?" He hiked his thumb over his shoulder. "I can go slower this time."

I scrunched my mouth to the side to keep from laughing. "Nah. I'm good, but thanks." I was still attracted to him—*big time*—there was no use denying that, but it didn't matter. We'd had our fun and the consequences of that had reared up and slapped us in the face. It didn't matter that he made my knees feel like jelly or caused my pulse to race. It was like Rae had said . . . it wasn't about us anymore. We had another life to consider.

Those rich brown eyes skated over my features, growing serious as he looked me over. "You look good. Your color's back."

"Thanks. I feel a lot better."

He nodded, pulling in a deep breath through his nose. "I'm glad, butterfly."

My belly swooped at his use of the nickname he'd given me during those months we'd been getting to know each other. He said it was because my wild nature had me flitting from one thing to the next, like a butterfly. When he used it at Rae and Zach's rehearsal, after he'd run out on me, it had hurt. But the pain seemed to have drifted away when I wasn't paying attention.

"I . . ." I paused, licking my lips and giving myself time to think through what I wanted to say. I didn't want to screw this up a second time. "About what I said last night—"

He lifted a hand and attempted to wave me off. "Hey, don't sweat it. Water under the bridge. Just forget about it."

"It's not though." I took a step forward, gripping the rung beneath the one he was leaning against, making the difference in our heights all the more obvious. That was one of the things I'd always loved about him; how he towered over me. "I don't want to forget about it. I want to apologize."

His brows dipped in at the center, but he remained silent. His chest stopped moving, and I got the impression he was holding his breath as he waited to see what I might say next.

"I'm sorry, Connor. What I said last night . . ." I shook my head. "It came out all wrong. I don't think you're a piece of shit. I don't think you'd abandon your responsibilities or bail on your child," I said, repeating the words he'd used from the night before. "I could never think that. You might have hurt me, but . . . I feel like I know the real you, deep down."

"You do," he said quickly, his fingers gripping the metal tight enough to turn his knuckles white. "You do know me, Ivy."

I nodded and inhaled deeply, holding it for a beat before blowing it back out. "I think you're going to be a great dad, Connor." His chin jerked back in shock, but I pushed on, wanting to get it all out there. "I think, if we put all the shit from the past aside, we can make this work."

His lips parted on a shaky exhale right before a slow smile creeped across his lips, stretching them wide until he was smiling at me so beautifully it made my legs shaky. God, it really should have been criminal how gorgeous his smile was.

"You do?"

"Yeah. There's no reason we can't do this, right?"

"Not at all."

Relief made my shoulders slump. "Great! So you agree, then. We can be friends and co-parent this kid together."

Some of the brilliance faded from his smile as the corners of his lips dipped. For a second I thought I might have read the situation wrong, but then he blinked and nodded. "For sure. Yeah. Total agreement."

Thank God. "The logistics might be a little hard to work out. I mean, I know your job keeps you on the road a lot, but—"

"I'm stayin'."

"I—" I rocked back on a heel. "What?"

"I'm stayin'. I'm movin' to Hope Valley."

"But . . . what about bull riding?"

He roughed a hand over his jaw and stared off to the side like he was giving my question some thought. "I lived on the road the way I did mainly because I didn't have any responsibilities keepin' me in one place. Obviously, that's changed now." He waved a hand toward my stomach. "I can have my home base wherever I want and travel to the different events I'm competing in, and I want that home base to be here."

I wasn't sure what I'd been expecting him to say, but it sure as hell hadn't been that. "Oh."

"I want to be a part of this baby's life, Ivy. I want to be a part of your pregnancy." His shoulders squared and his chin lifted, and I watched in awe as determination slid over his massive frame. "I want to prove to you that I'm in this. One hundred percent."

I didn't realize until that very moment how badly I'd needed that reassurance from him. "Okay," I said quietly.

He nodded, his features growing resolute. "So we're in agreement."

"Right."

"Great. So I'll move in this weekend."

"Alright—wait. *What?*"

He smiled, and I knew I'd somehow played right into the bastard's hand. "I told you I wanted to be a part of this. The best way to do that is to be close to you. The best way to be close to you is by living together. So I'm moving in."

"The hell you are!" I shrieked.

He reached over the railing and brushed his thumb across my jaw in a soothing gesture. "Shh, sweetheart. You can't go gettin' worked up over every little thing. It's not good for the baby."

Oh, that son of a bitch. I clenched my hands and

stomped my foot as I demanded, "You are *not* moving in with me."

He lifted a shoulder, the picture of calm and casual. "We'll see. Now, if you'll excuse me, I need to get back to work."

He turned around and headed toward the horse, leaving me so steamed I couldn't appreciate watching his ass as he walked away.

I was going to murder him.

Chapter Twenty

IVY

"How did this even happen?" Lennix asked as she stared out my back window, watching as Connor hauled a duffle bag stuffed so full it looked like it was about to split at the seams out of the bed of his truck, hooking the strap over his shoulder before heading for the carriage house-turned apartment at the back of my property.

"This was the compromise we came up with," I muttered around the rim of my teacup. I'd discovered recently that peppermint tea helped settle my stomach, so I made sure to always keep some on hand. "It was the carriage house or I kill him in his sleep. I went with the option that didn't come with jail time."

Lennix's laugh brought a smile to my face. I might grumble and put on a show that I wasn't okay with

Connor moving into my carriage house, but the truth was, knowing he'd be close put me at ease. As excited as I was for this little chickpea, I was also scared. I made the mistake of googling pregnancy and had fallen down a rabbit hole of all the things that could possibly go wrong. The pregnancy had started to feel a little isolating after that, especially since I hadn't told my parents yet, but now that Connor was here I didn't feel so alone.

I drew the line at him living in the main house with me, however. That would have been like dumping a bag of candy on the floor in front of a group of kids and telling them they could look, but they couldn't touch or eat any.

It had only been two days since Connor and I had talked, and in that short amount of time it felt like a switch had been flipped inside of me. All of a sudden the exhaustion that had been plaguing me let up. My energy started to return, which I was excited for, but another change that had occurred recently that was more . . . problematic.

All of a sudden I couldn't stop thinking about sex.

It started the other night when I was curled up on the couch, watching a movie on Netflix. At one point the couple on the screen started to kiss, and as the scene got steamier, my body got hotter. In the past two days, I'd given my vibrator a workout like it hadn't seen in months. I felt like a teenage boy, for Christ's sake. A stiff wind would perk my nipples right up. It was ridiculous.

Connor and I had agreed we would co-parent this baby as friends once it finally arrived, and the last thing I wanted to do was put that in jeopardy because my stupid hormones made me want to latch onto him like a freaking koala.

It certainly didn't help matters that my new sort-of-roomie had a face and body that looked like they'd been chiseled out of granite. I blamed him. It was his fault he was so freaking gorgeous.

"Well, this is an improvement, right? I mean, at least you guys are getting along, and you aren't sad or rage-y anymore."

No, I was stupidly horny. But she didn't need to know that.

"Right. Exactly. If we can keep getting along for the sake of the baby, maybe this will all work out."

Lennix moved away from the window and came to sit across from me at the kitchen table. It was another Aunt Sylvia piece I'd kept because it was absolutely beautiful. She'd used broken stoneware and vases to create a colorful mosaic that was as much a work of art as it was a sturdy piece of furniture.

On that thought I realized I was going to be raising the next generation of the Young family in this very house that had seen so much love. It had started with Sylvia, then my mom, then me, and now my little chickpea. I was sure

Sylvia was looking down on me, smiling and happy to know the house she had filled with love was going to get a new member soon enough.

My mom would be happy too. Just as soon as I found the guts to tell her. Micah was going to be a different story. He would be happy . . . eventually. And he would love this baby because he loved me. But I couldn't be certain that Connor wouldn't go missing one day and end up as a *Dateline* special or the focus of a true crime podcast.

He'd always had my back growing up, no matter the kind of scrapes I got myself in, and there was a tiny part of me that worried this might be the scrape he couldn't bring himself to look past.

"Have you scheduled an appointment with an obstetrician yet?"

I nodded and sipped more tea, the sweet, minty flavor warming me from the inside. "Yeah. I got in with one here in town. We go see her on Monday."

Lennix hiked her eyebrows high on her forehead. "*We*?"

I gave her a flat look. "Yes, *we*. I told you, Connor said he wanted to be a part of this. I told him about the appointment and he insisted on being there."

She reached across the table and took my hand in hers, giving it a squeeze. "Are you excited?"

"I am." I blew out a sigh and admitted, "But I'm

nervous too. I was really sick for a while. What if that hurt the baby somehow?"

She smiled reassuringly. "Everything's going to be perfect. You'll see. You and that little tadpole are doing just fine. And in a matter of months, you're going to have a little baby," she finished on a squeak of excitement. "A tiny little wild child bull rider. Honestly, Ivy, this baby might end up being the hottest baby to ever be born in this town."

I let out a bubble of laughter. "I don't think you can refer to a baby as hot."

She waved me off and blew out a raspberry. "*Pfft*, whatever. You know I'm right. You're freaking gorgeous, and Connor's hotter than the flames in hell. It's like, a scientific fact your baby is going to be beautiful."

I pointed a finger in her direction. "Or it could go the opposite way," I said in warning. "You know, like all those beautiful celebrities who have babies that look less like them and more like their third cousin twice removed who got kicked in the head by a mule and has the unfortunate hairline that goes all the way to their unibrow."

Lennix burst out laughing, and I quickly joined in. "Nah. That won't happen to you. That's karma because all those celebrities are secretly terrible people. You're a good person, so your baby won't be punished."

That might have been one of the most ridiculous

conversations I'd had in my life, but the laughter was just what I needed, and by the time Lennix left later that evening, I felt a sense of peace that had been missing for a while.

It was amazing what good friends were capable of.

I FIDGETED IN THE PASSENGER SEAT OF CONNOR'S truck as he guided us through town toward the doctor's office. I caught him glance my way every couple minutes like he was trying to gage my mood as I stared out the windshield chewing on my thumbnail.

"You know this is all going to be good, right?" He finally spoke up after parking at the clinic and coming around my side of the truck to help me out. "I know you're nervous, but it's all going to work out."

I dropped my hand and wiped my sweaty palms on the thighs of my jeans. "I know," I said on a gust of air. "I know, you're right. But I don't think I'm going to be settled until I see it with my own eyes, you know?"

He smiled down at me. It wasn't his charming smile or the one he used on camera for interviews or in that one underwear campaign he did that I might have printed out and kept stashed in the drawer of my bedside table.

"I've got you." Three simple words, yet the surety in his voice when he said them as he reached up and caressed my arms in soothing, gentle strokes, worked wonders in grounding me. "You aren't alone, okay? I'm right here, and I'm going to make sure everything is okay."

I took my first full breath that day and returned his smile. "Thanks."

"Don't have to thank me for doin' my job, sweetheart. Now, you ready?" He held his hand out and waited for me to place my palm in his.

I gave him a single sharp nod once his fingers wrapped around mine securely and together.

Hi. I'm Ivy Young, I'm here for my appointment with Dr. Shaundry."

The woman behind the front desk lifted her head, and her eyes went wide with recognition. "Oh, hi."

My smile shook a little as I looked back at Blythe. "Hi." I hadn't seen her since that time at Muffin Top a few months back, despite my attempts to call and connect. She was always incredibly polite, just stressed that she was busy with work and the kids. I understood. She was a single mom of three now, since her husband passed. I hoped she wasn't closing herself off from everything else.

She looked a lot better than she had when she'd first

gotten back into town, but I could still see the haunting sadness in her eyes, and it broke my heart for her. "I didn't realize you were working here."

"Yeah. For about a month and a half now."

"And you like it?" As far as small talk went, it wasn't my finest attempt, but I'd already locked in, so I was determined to see it through.

"Oh, yeah. It's good. And Dr. Shaundry is great," she added quickly, as though it were an afterthought. "You're in good hands."

I swallowed. "Thanks. Um . . ." I looked around the seating area, thankful it was empty, aside from Connor and me. Leaning in, I lowered my voice so only she could hear me. "Um, no one else knows about . . ." I waved my hand in front of my midsection awkwardly. "If you wouldn't mind not mentioning you saw me here? I'm telling my parents tonight. I just . . . I wanted to make sure everything is okay first."

"Of course!" she insisted. "I wouldn't say anything. But, um . . ." She cast a look over my shoulder to where Connor was sitting in one of the chairs that was too small for his frame. "Congratulations." Her smile grew a bit warmer. "You're going to be a great mom, Ivy."

I returned her smile and reached over the desk to give her hand a squeeze. "Thanks." With that done, I turned and headed toward Connor, taking the empty seat beside him. He looked up from the magazine he was thumbing through with a furrowed brow. "Everything okay?"

"Yeah. It's good." I cast my eyes at the magazine and back up to him. "Interesting reading?"

He shrugged and went back to reading, the picture of confidence holding a magazine on breastfeeding. "I'm reading whatever I can get my hands on. I want to make sure I'm prepared by the time chickpea gets here."

Two things hit me at once. The first was that I loved how he heard me refer to the baby as *chickpea* and had adopted the moniker as well. The second was the knowledge that he'd been studying up on all things baby so he could be prepared. It was a blow so hard to that protective wall around my heart it damaged the structural integrity. I wasn't sure how many more hits like that I could withstand.

"You're studying?"

"I wouldn't call it studying. It's not like I'm preparing for a test. I think every new father should know as much as humanly possible in order to help the mom in any way she might need."

Bam! Hit number two.

And, *son of a bitch,* but every word out of his mouth only made him sexier. I wasn't sure my vibrator was strong enough to survive the workout it was going to get later tonight.

Fortunately, I was saved from my naughty gutter thoughts when a nurse opened the door to the back and popped her head out, calling my name.

Blythe had been right. Dr. Shaundry was great. I'd told her my concerns—thanks a lot, *Google* and *WebMd*—and she hadn't looked at me like I was crazy once. She patiently explained away every one of my fears, putting me at ease so I could finally focus on my excitement. I hadn't expected it but Connor had some questions too, and they were surprisingly astute, and things I wouldn't have thought to ask. Thanks to him, I now knew I wasn't allowed to go near a charcuterie board or sushi for the foreseeable future. I wasn't sure if I appreciated him looking out for me or pissed off that, because of him, I had to avoid two of my favorite things for the next several months. At the moment I was leaning toward pissed.

"What do you say, guys? You ready to see your baby?" Dr. Shaundry asked, interrupting my mourning for my beloved spicy tuna roll.

"We get to see it now?" Connor asked, his voice full of awe. "It's not too soon?"

She shook her head. "Nope. Not too soon. We won't

be able to tell the gender yet, but I can take measurements, and if your little one cooperates, we should be able to see the heartbeat."

She instructed me to place my feet in the stirrups on the bed and squirted jelly on a long, weird-looking wand before inserting it. Definitely not the most comfortable situation I'd ever been in, but the discomfort only lasted as long as it took for her to point at a little white speck on the monitor beside her.

"Ah, there it is."

"Where?" Connor and I asked at the same time.

She drew a circle with her finger. "Right here. That's your baby."

"Wow." At the wonder in Connor's voice, I turned my head to look up at him. His gaze was glued to the screen, his lips partially separated, and I could have sworn his eyes grew damp. "That's our baby," he whispered softly.

Bam! Hit number three.

"And that flutter right there is the heartbeat."

My head whipped back around to the screen to see where she was pointing. "You can see the heartbeat?"

The doctor smiled. "Yep. And you can hear it too if you want."

"Please," I answered quickly.

She pushed a few buttons, and a second later the room filled with a sound similar to rushing water. It was a soft *whom, whom, whom* that was, hands down, the most beautiful thing I had ever heard.

"Oh my God," I breathed as I looked back up at Connor with a watery laugh. "That's our baby's heartbeat."

"Sure is, and it sounds strong. Everything with your little one is absolutely perfect."

Connor closed his eyes and pulled in a breath before taking my hand in his and leaning in to press his forehead against mine. "Absolutely perfect," he repeated in a hushed voice full of relief.

Bam. Hit number four.

Ivy was flitting around the first floor of her house like a butterfly, but this time, instead of being wild and fun, she was more . . . hyperactive and anxious.

"You really need to relax, sweetheart. You're stressed about nothin'."

I knew from the murderous scowl she shot in my direction I'd just said the wrong thing, but I didn't know what else to say or do to help calm her down. It had been a week since the ultrasound. For most of those few days we'd been riding a high. I knew I was. I mean, how could I not. I heard my baby's freaking *heartbeat*.

It had to have been the coolest experience of my life. I got to hear the heartbeat of a life I helped create. A little chickpea that was half mine and half the woman I was steadily falling for on a daily basis. There was no other person on the planet I would have wanted to experience that with. The moment the room filled with that echo-y whooshing sound I knew what true, unfiltered happiness was.

I wished it had been something I could have talked about with my parents in person. After all, it had taken a while to guide them through the shell shock at discovering they were going to be grandparents. It was something my mom had harped on me about for quite some time now, but in her head it was with a woman I was in a loving, committed relationship with. Marriage or not, she didn't care as long as we were happy. But learning over the phone it was the result of a drunken night after a wedding had been a bit of a blow. It had helped a bit when she learned I had real feelings for Ivy and that, despite the stupid agreement we had to co-parent as friends—I was really starting to hate that word—I was secretly trying win her back. I just had to be sly about it. I couldn't let on that I woke every morning with the sole purpose of worming my way beneath her skin and back into her heart.

When we talked about the baby, I'd actually choked up as I tried to put into words how I felt at seeing that little flutter on the screen. Hearing that had set off my mother's waterworks and she spent the rest of that phone call in happy tears. I'd promised them both they would get to meet Ivy soon enough, and there wasn't a doubt in my mind they were going to love her. She was exactly the type of crazy my tattoo artist mother would connect with, and her business savvy and work ethic were something my attorney father would respect.

Now, after a week of great, she was, once again, a nervous wreck.

She pushed her chin out and blew a puff of air upward to try and blow a lock of hair out of her face. "I really think it would be for the best if you let me break the news to them alone."

I placed the basket of dinner rolls in the center of the dining room table and turned to her to tuck the hair behind her ears so it would quit bothering her. "I told you, that's not gonna happen."

She was finally going to tell her mom and stepdad about the pregnancy, and she decided the best way to do that was over a homecooked family dinner. When I informed her that I planned on being there when she told them, she'd cracked up for a solid minute and a half. When she realized I wasn't kidding, she panicked. She spent the better part of the day trying to convince me it was a bad idea, and her list of reasons was substantial. Starting with her cop stepdad killing me and ending with the likelihood of my body never being found.

I wasn't worried.

My resolve to fight for the woman I wanted hadn't

lessened. If anything, after that doctor's appointment it had grown that much stronger. I was in this to win, and I wouldn't be scared off by anyone.

I took the linen napkin she'd been folding and re-folding for the past five minutes and set it aside. Reaching up, I placed my hands on either side of her neck and used my thumbs to tilt her face up as I crouched to bring myself eye-level with her. I wasn't making a conscious effort to touch her any chance I could get, it was just something I couldn't help. I did it without thinking, my body drawn to hers whenever she was around. If she was close enough, my hands sought her out in some way.

"I promise, tonight is going to be great."

She let out an indelicate snort. "You can't possibly promise something like that."

"I can. I told you already that I've got you, I'll make sure everything is fine, and I mean it." I wasn't going to let anyone stress Ivy out more than she already was. I wouldn't let anyone make her feel bad or ashamed about the situation we were in. Not even her own family.

"I think I could soften the blow a bit before they meet you. That way they have some time to wrap their head around everything."

I stroked the side of her neck with the pad of my thumb, not missing the way her pupils expanded or the slight lean of her body to get a little closer to my touch. It was those little signs that she still wanted me—or at least her body did—that kept me going. Kept me hoping.

"Nope. We're in this together. We're a team, remember? We do this together or not at all."

She blew out a raspberry and took a step back, breaking our connection as she ran her hands down the front of her shirt. When I arrived earlier to help her prepare for dinner and got my first glimpse of her in a pair of painted-on jeans and a vintage concert tee that left an inch of bare, creamy skin visible along her stomach and back, I'd gone instantly hard. The past week and a half had been a true test of strength for me. Living so damn close to her but still being too far from her was driving me out of my goddamn mind.

More than once, I'd woken up and shuffled into my small kitchenette for my morning coffee only to spot her through the window of her house still dressed in her pajamas with her hair wild and her face soft with sleep. The woman slept in these slinky, satin-y nighties that would cause a priest to question his vow of celibacy, and I was nowhere near as restrained as a man of the cloth.

If it wasn't those goddamn nighties, it was the skin-tight spandex she wore when she did yoga beside her back garden.

I'd pumped my own dick so much lately that I was starting to worry about blisters.

"Stop fidgeting," I told her, silently willing my dick not to get hard tonight. "You look beautiful."

"My boobs look ridiculous," she grumbled as she looked down at her chest and grabbed the body parts in question, lifting them up and letting them drop again. *So much for not getting hard.* "I swear to God they've gotten bigger. What do you think?" She looked up at me guilelessly. "Do they look bigger to you?"

I let out a pained groan and dropped my head back. "I think I'm not above beggin' you to please not talk about your tits. The last thing we need is for me to meet your folks sporting a half-chub."

Her eyes darted down to my dick and the tip of her tongue peeked out to swipe across her bottom lip before she pulled it between her teeth and bit down.

"Fuckin' hell," I growled. "You can't look at me like that. It's not helping."

Her eyes bulged out as they darted back up to my face. "Sorry," she squeaked, her cheeks staining pink. "I'm sorry."

The doorbell rang a moment later, and I wasn't sure if I was grateful for the interruption or pissed off. I didn't have time to decide, because Ivy was scurrying to the door and grabbing the knob before the chime had even stopped.

I stood between the dining room and kitchen with my hands stuffed into the pockets of my jeans as I waited patiently. Truth be told, I was nervous as hell. I hadn't done the whole "meet the parents" thing in a really long time, and I would have been lying if I said I wasn't worried about making a good impression. But I kept that from Ivy, wanting to be a rock for her to lean on, not another cause of stress.

"Hey, love bug!" I heard just before a set of arms wrapped around Ivy and pulled her into an embrace.

"Hey, Mom." I could hear the affection Ivy held for her mom in her voice.

"Missed you, Monster," a male voice greeted, making my little butterfly laugh.

"Hi, Mike. Missed you too." She stepped back and waved her folks in. "Come on in, guys. There's actually someone here I want you to meet."

If ever there was a time for me to shine, it was this one.

Christ, I hoped I didn't shit my pants the one time it mattered the most.

Ivy

. . .

"You want us to meet someone?" My mom's brows went up in curiosity while Micah's dipped down in an unhappy frown.

"Thought this was family dinner?" Micah grumbled. "Who would you want us to meet at a family dinner?" he asked, putting extra emphasis on the word family.

I laughed nervously. "Well, it's funny you should ask that." *Just do it and get it over with*, I told myself. The faster the better. Like ripping a wax strip off your bikini area. I lifted my arm, indicating Connor as they stepped into the house, shutting the door behind them. Connor waved politely and stayed in place as though waiting for my cue. "I don't know if you guys remember Connor Bennett from Rae and Zach's wedding?"

"Of course." My mom smiled politely and walked to him, shaking his hand. "It's nice to see you again."

Micah offered him a silent chin lift in that weird way guys did.

"Well, Connor's here because . . . I'm pregnant. And he's the father."

Riiiiiip.

THE SILENCE AROUND THE TABLE WAS LIKE AN uninvited fifth dinner companion. The creepy uncle who was never invited places because he weirded everyone out.

Or that one aunt who insisted on kissing everyone on the mouth.

The only sound that filled the otherwise deafening quiet was the clink of silverware against dishes as we ate. The few bites I'd taken sat like a brick in my stomach.

After ten agonizing minutes, Connor broke the silence. "This is really good, butterfly."

My stepfather slapped his napkin down on the table. "I'm gonna murder your ass."

Oh goody. Everyone was talking again.

My mom reached over and put a calming hand on her husband's arm. "Will you relax? You aren't going to kill anyone."

"Am too. I'm gonna kill him." Micah picked up his fork and held it in his fist like he would a hunting knife, the gesture meant to be threatening.

Used to ignoring her husband's ridiculous antics, my mother looked at me with a gentle smile. "It all makes sense now. No wonder you were so sick before. I should have known. When I first got pregnant with you I couldn't keep anything down."

I leaned forward and braced my chin on my fist, eager to hear stories about when my mother was pregnant. "Really?"

"Yeah." She nodded on a laugh. "Your grandmother went through the same thing. She said it was the fiery hair.

Made morning sickness even worse. I didn't believe her, of course. But then you were born, and, well . . ." She waved her hand at my strawberry hued hair.

"So you think I'll have a little redhead too?" The thought made me smile.

Mom returned my dreamy look. "Wouldn't that be something?"

"I think I'd like a little redheaded girl, just like her mom," Connor said, his dimples coming out and pointing right at me.

"You don't talk," Micah barked at him. "This is all your *damn* fault, so you sit there quietly and eat your *damn* dinner."

I heaved out a sigh. "Mike, will you please quit threatening him?"

"Is it Mike?" Connor's confused gaze darted between me and my mother. "I thought it was Micah."

I opened my mouth to respond, but of course Micah beat me to it. "Only Ivy calls me Mike," he bit out. "You can call me Mr. Langford. Or *Lieutenant*." He hooked a brow upward. "Tell me, *Connor*. You got any outstanding warrants? You wanted in any other state? What's your criminal history look like? You a drinker? A gambler?"

"Ignore him, please," I said to Connor, rolling my eyes at my stepfather's ridiculousness. "His name is Micah. I called him Mike when I was little. The nickname sort of stuck."

He crossed his arms over his chest and glared Connor down. "And you're not allowed to use it."

Good lord, was he pouting?

I tossed my napkin down and pushed away from the table. Stomping into the kitchen, I snatched the sonogram off the fridge and brought it back into the dining room. I handed it to my mother. "I'm a little over nine weeks."

"Oh my God," she breathed, her eyes growing damp and her hand coming up to cover her mouth as she looked at my little baby blip in the picture. "Look at that." She sniffled. "My baby is having a baby."

"Look, I know this didn't happen the traditional way, but it happened." I cut my eyes to Micah. "I'm not a kid, I'm a consenting adult. Connor and I did everything we were supposed to do to prevent this. It happened anyway."

Micah's face grew red, and I was willing to bet he wanted to slap his hands over his ears and shout *la la la la la*.

"I'm keeping the baby. Connor and I have talked about it, and we are going to co-parent. He moved into Sylvia's carriage house to be close. We might not be doing things the way people would expect, but we're going to make it work. We're going to love this baby and we're going to make sure it's happy. How we do it is going to look a little different from the norm."

Connor reached over and took my hand in his, lending me his strength. I'd been wrong for suggesting he not be here for this, and I was so glad he hadn't listened to me. Having him here made this easier. Made me feel stronger. I smiled at him, mouthing a silent *thank you.*

He shot me a wink that I felt in my clit, but I pushed the sensation away and looked back at my parents. "Do you guys have any questions for us?"

Dinner went a bit smoother after that. While Micah never stopped staring daggers at Connor, he at least quit with the verbal threats. When Mom pointed out the baby in the sonogram picture, I watched as he visibly melted, staring at Chickpea in a way I could only describe as proud grandpa.

Mom told us more stories from her pregnancy, which gave way to telling Connor about some of the crazy things I'd gotten up to when I was a little girl. By the time dinner was over my stress was gone. My mother pulled Connor into an affectionate hug, welcoming him into the family.

When I walked them to the door, Micah hung back after my mom and I shared our goodbyes and she headed to the car.

He cleared his throat uncomfortably and tugged at his collar. "Look, I know I'm not your biological dad, but blood has never mattered to me. I want you to know, you're my daughter. No matter what. And if you ever need anything, I'm always here."

I launched myself at the man who had cherished me as his own from the moment he met me as a four-year-old, dressed in a mud-covered tutu, a glittery skull shirt, and sparkly combat boots. "You're my dad," I whispered into his neck. "Always will be."

He squeezed me tightly. "Love you with all my heart, Monster," he whispered into my hair.

"And I love you with all of mine." I pulled back and placed a kiss to his cheek, dashing at the tear that had spilled free with the back of my hand before placing it on my belly. "And I'm so happy this baby is going to have you as a grandpa."

He sniffed and cleared his throat. "Well . . . okay then. Enough of this emotional stuff, yeah? I better get your mom home. We'll talk soon."

I shut the door and turned around to press my back against it, a smile taking over my face. When I looked in the direction of the dining room, I saw the table had been mostly cleared, and I could hear the sound of running water and the clink of dishes coming from the kitchen where Connor had taken it upon himself to clean up.

Bam. Another direct hit.

The air smelled like a combination of fried food, beer, and animals, which, to some people might have been a combination that would turn your stomach, but I liked it. I didn't know if it was the pregnancy or what, but the smell actually made me kind of hungry.

The sounds of carnival rides and loud, rowdy kids caused me to smile as I made my way through the fairgrounds. I ripped off a big chunk of the sugary funnel cake I was carrying on a flimsy paper plate and popped it into my mouth, chewing with delight.

I'd lived in a small town most of my life, but this was my first time ever going to a rodeo. Until Connor, I'd never even watched any of the events on TV. But when he told me last week that there was a rodeo about an hour from Hope Valley he was competing in and asked if I would come to watch him ride, I quickly said yes.

The past few weeks had been going so well. It felt like Connor and I were rediscovering the friendship we'd first built so long ago. He was the best sort-of-roommate I'd ever had. He showed up at my back door regularly with strawberry cheese Danishes and caffeine free lattes from Muffin Top. He took it upon himself to mow the yard. And there was even one afternoon when I found him up in my old treehouse, prying boards loose. When I rushed out to ask him what he was doing, he said he was replacing the broken or rotted wood so the treehouse would be safe for our kid to use it when they were old enough.

At that point I'd given up trying to keep that protective wall standing.

We had dinner together more nights than not, unless he was out of town for a rodeo or stuck working late at Safe Haven Ranch, and the more time I spent with him, the more I was starting to like him all over again. I'd forgotten how easy his company was, but now with the pregnancy, he'd taken it to a whole new level. He was attentive and considerate and thoughtful. Twice he'd shown up with groceries, fully restocking my fridge and pantry without me having to ask, so if I could show him even an ounce of the support he'd been showing me the past few weeks, I wanted to do it.

When Rae and Lennix found out my plans for the weekend, they'd decided to tag along, dragging Raylan and Zach along with them.

A group of screaming kids ran past, kicking up dust in their hurry to get to wherever they were going. "Ooh, did you see that?" I swallowed the mouthful of fried dough and licked my lips, my craving turning on a dime. "That one kid had a giant turkey leg. Did anyone see where we can get the turkey legs?"

Lennix started cracking up and Rae just glared.

"Wha?" I muttered around another heaping bite of funnel cake.

Her eyes scanned me up and down before narrowing even farther. "Where do you even put all this food, you bitch?"

I snorted, nearly sending powdered sugar out of my nose. I was officially in my twelfth week of pregnancy, and with it came the weirdest food cravings. I'd been standing in the open door of my fridge the other day, crunching on a pickle like people so often did, when I had the thought, *hey*! *I bet this would taste awesome with mustard on it.*

Breaking news: it did.

Pregnant Ivy was a culinary genius.

"My boobs," I mumbled around fried, sugar-coated bread. And wasn't that the damn truth? You might not have been able to tell I was pregnant by looking at me, but my boobs had gotten *insane*. And my nipples were so freaking sensitive.

"Jeez, don't remind me." Lennix looked longingly at my chest before staring down at hers. "I'm so freaking jealous right now."

Zach let out an uncomfortable cough, twisting around so his eyes trailed after Turkey Leg Kid. "I think I saw a sign for them a few booths back." He hiked a thumb over his shoulder. "Think I'll go check it out."

"For the love of all that's holy, take me with you," Raylan grumbled, following after him.

"Grab a turkey leg for me!" I shouted after them as they disappeared from sight, getting swallowed up by the large groups of people.

I checked the time on my phone. "The rodeo should be starting soon. We should probably head over."

We made our way from the fairgrounds over to the arena where the events were held, and I was surprised to see just how big the whole setup was. The stands were already filling up quickly, so the three of us hustled to find seats. So far I'd had a lot of fun, and I was excited to get to watch Connor ride in person.

Things got underway and I was swept up in the energy of it all. I really liked the barrel racing, saddle bronc riding, and the steer roping. I wasn't huge on the steer wrestling, mainly because it looked like it hurt those poor animals' necks, but Lennix assured me they were all fine.

"Oh, this is the event Zach used to compete in, she pointed out to Rae and me just as the tie-down roping kicked off.

Zach and Raylan made it back to us—turkey legs in hand—right before the bull riding kicked off. Anticipation thrummed in my veins as I watched one rider after another. The excitement in the arena was infectious, and I soaked it up like a sponge, letting it wash over me as I munched on my turkey leg and pressed my hand to my belly. There was no way Chickpea was cognizant of, well, anything, actually, but it still sort of felt like the two of us were here to support Daddy in his job.

I didn't know all that much about bull riding, and I couldn't tell you whether or not any of the guys I'd watched so far had ridden well or not, but it had been impressive, though I didn't get the same thrill watching them as I did every time I'd watched Connor on TV or YouTube. Given the adrenaline rush I was experiencing then, I could only imagine how it felt for him. He had to have been buzzing with it.

About halfway through the announcer called out a

name that had at least half the crowd on their feet cheering and clapping. Apparently this Vance Grimes dude was a crowd favorite. When I lifted my hands to clap for the next rider, Zach quickly reached over and stopped me. He shook his head when I looked over at him quizzically. "We don't like that guy," he told me ominously.

"Why not?"

"Just ask Connor. He'll tell you."

With that cryptic explanation, we faced the arena as the gate flew open and the bull surged out, thrashing violently and rattling around the guy on its back like a ragdoll.

People all around me hooted and hollered, and when the buzzer finally sounded and the rider hopped off, I caught a glimpse of why Connor might not have cared for the guy. As the bullfighters rushed into the arena to chase the bull out, the rider showboated and hammed it up for the crowd. He even held his hand up to his ear and waved them on when the crowd started cheering his name to keep them going and feed his ego.

His smile was too arrogant for my liking and he appeared too polished for a job that consisted of getting on the back of a dirty animal for eight seconds before being tossed in the dirt. I mean, the guy's hair was gelled into place, for crying out loud. And from where I sat in the stands, I could see that his teeth looked unnaturally white and comically large. Whoever had done this dude's veneers should be fired. This guy's appearance mattered a great deal to him. He was attractive and he knew it, and if I had to guess, he expected those around him to acknowledge it.

When he was finished receiving adoration from his fans, he sauntered over to the fence and hopped up, leaning over to lock lips with a busty brunette hanging over from the other side. The camera that reflected on the big screen at the end of the arena panned in on the couple just as the kiss went from congratulatory to inappropriate-for-children-to-see. And when they finally broke apart, they didn't appear to care that they'd just given everyone a show they might not have wanted to watch.

I turned away from the couple and looked back at the chute to watch the next rider, and a second later my eyes homed in on a familiar figure climbing onto the top of the metal fence next to the chute.

The moisture was sucked out of my mouth at the sight of Connor in all his bull-rider glory. He had on Wranglers, only this time he wore a pair of brown leather chaps over them that accentuated his ass and thick thighs. And *dayum*, but the man could wear the shit out of a pair of chaps. He wore a padded vest over his chambray shirt that did nothing to hide the bulk and power of his shoulders and arms.

"What's he doing?" I leaned over and whispered to

Zach as Connor started talking to the guy who'd climbed onto the back of the bull banging around in the chute.

"Kid riding next is new to the circuit," he started to explain. "Connor's givin' him some tips so he has a better ride."

My heart stutter-stepped as I watched Connor's arms move animatedly as he said something to the guy in the chute. "Does he do that a lot? Help other riders, I mean?"

Zach nodded. "He's been at this a long time. Has the knowledge and likes to share it with the younger riders to help them improve. He said once that there's no point in bein' the best if there's no real competition. He wants to make sure the guys he goes up against know their shit. That way, if he beats them, he knows he earned it. Plus, he just likes helpin' out."

I slowly faced forward and parted my lips, letting out a shaky exhale as my core began to throb. I shouldn't have thought that was sexy, but damn it, I did. My voice came out throatier than normal as I asked, "And is he? The best?"

Zach looked at me with a crooked smile and nodded. "Yep. Guy that just rode is right behind him in ranking, but can't seem to push himself over. He can't stand Connor 'cause he knows he's better but doesn't want to admit it."

"Ah." So that explained why we didn't like the guy. He was a cocky asshole.

The gate opened and I went back to watching as the guy Connor had instructed held himself on the bull, dead set on tossing him right out of the arena, with nothing but sheer determination. Then I watched as the buzzer sounded and Connor stood up on the fence, cupping his hands around his mouth and whooping for the kid before clapping proudly and cheering him on.

Turned out, Connor was the last rider of the evening, right after the kid he'd helped. I didn't know if it was my imagination, or if the bull he'd pulled was a meaner bastard than all the others, but as the animal beat itself against the metal panels of the chute, a flurry of nervousness filled my stomach.

If I thought the crowd got loud for that Vance guy, it was nothing compared to how they went positively feral for Connor.

My heart started to race as Connor gingerly lowered himself onto the beast, sucking in a sharp gasp when he was thrashed around a little bit.

"It's all good, Ivy," Zach reassured me. "He's got this. Drew the best bull of the night."

Well, that answered that. I knew enough to know that drawing the best bull meant you basically got an animal who wants to maim and murder you. The bull

Connor was clinging to was, in fact, meaner than all the others.

I held my breath and sent up a silent prayer as Connor secured his hand with the rope, giving it a few testing tugs before nodding, then the gate flew open with a crash and the bull went charging out, the father of my baby attached to its back.

Eight seconds felt like an eternity. The noise in the arena was deafening as nearly everyone surged to their feet. I followed suit, clasping my hands over my mouth and watching with wide-eyed fascination as Connor's hips moved in time with every buck and twist of the animal beneath him, almost as if he could anticipate its movements before it made them. He was fluid, a rolling wave. A thing of beauty. It didn't take a genius to understand why he was the best. You had to watch him close enough and you'd see it.

The buzzer sounded and the noise went from deafening to straight up insanity. I was yelling so loudly my throat started to hurt as Connor untangled his hand from the rope and launched himself to the ground. Where that Vance asshole preened like a peacock for attention, my man oozed big dick energy without even trying.

Wait, no . . . not *my* man.

I shook that thought away and watched Connor dominate the arena. It was so slight most people wouldn't have noticed, but as someone who'd been watching Connor like a creeper the past couple of weeks, I didn't miss the way the knee he'd injured the year prior buckled a little more than the other when he landed, or the wince on his face before he quickly schooled his features.

And I couldn't help but wonder if Connor had been keeping a secret that could potentially get him seriously hurt . . . or worse.

Adrenaline was still pumping through my entire body after that ride, and all I could think about was getting to Ivy. I hadn't felt this good after a ride, this exhilarated, in years. It almost felt like it used to when I was younger. When I still loved rodeoing more than anything. When I'd had an incredible ride and the high stuck around for hours afterward.

Back then, the rodeo grounds were the only place I could imagine being, basking in the accolades of the people who'd come to watch me. I thrived on the back slaps and congratulations. On the buckles and the purse, knowing I'd taken home more money in those eight seconds than some people did at their jobs for months. Back then the sponsors used to chase after me, kissing my ass for a chance to work with me. It was good to be Connor Bennett, the best bull rider on the circuit.

This was the closest I'd come to feeling the high of the old days, and she was the only reason. I knew she'd been in the stands watching me, and the need to impress her had been the driving force that had been missing for longer than I could remember.

I sat up on that fence earlier and scanned the crowd until I spotted her beautiful face. I memorized where she sat with our friends so I could find her again after the buzzer sounded, and when I spotted her on her feet yelling and whistling for me, my dick stood at attention, beating against my fly in time with my heartbeat as if to say *mine, mine, mine.* I couldn't remember the last time I'd had someone in the stands shouting for me, cheering me on the way she had. My parents tried to come to any rodeo I was at in Texas if it was close enough to Cloverleaf, but that was different. Not even Amber cheered for me with as much enthusiasm as my wild butterfly.

Amber had been too busy acting like she was some kind of fucking celebrity, the queen of the circuit or some shit, using my name for clout. She had loved me when my reputation had gotten her what she wanted. Same with Dusty. As long as he could brag about his young protégé, I was his favorite person. A streak of bad luck years back had changed their tune fast.

After that, I'd learned to block out the noise. Even when I found my footing again, I dulled the crowd. I did what I came to do, and I left. Sure, I put on a show that nothing had changed, that I was still the same old fun-loving, good time guy, but it wasn't the truth anymore. Hadn't been for a long time.

"Great ride, man."

"Hell of a good time watchin' you up there."

"You blew Grimes out of the water."

I gave my thanks to the other bull riders who stuck around to congratulate me as I wound my way through the crowd with one destination in mind. I needed to get to her.

I cleared the hallway that led down to the locker rooms and stepped out into the sunshine. It took no time at all to the find that beautiful rose-gold hair and the smiling sapphire eyes that went with it. She stood off to the side, leaning against the fence with our friends. I wanted to run right for her, scoop her up, and plant my lips against hers. But I couldn't do that. At least not yet. I was still playing her game. Pretending to be friends. Like I didn't want more.

Like I didn't want fucking *everything*.

"Hey," I said as I got closer, calling my crew's attention. Zach smiled, offering me a back-slapping hug. Raylan slapped my hand before yanking me in for a shoulder clap.

Lennix and Rae hugged me in congratulations, all of them incredibly excited for me. It felt good to win this one with all of them here to see it, but I was most excited for Ivy's reaction.

"That was incredible!" she squeaked, lifting on her tiptoes with her hands balled in front of her before she launched herself at me for a full-body hug. "Oh my God, that was so cool! Seeing you in person like that? You were amazing up there!" Her eyes glittered as she pulled back to look at me, and I made sure to keep my hands on her hips to keep her close for a few more seconds, not ready to let her go or break contact yet.

I smiled big, putting those dimples on display because I knew how much she liked them. I was fighting dirty, and I didn't feel the slightest bit bad for it. I fully intended to use every tool and weapon in my arsenal to win her back. If the past few weeks had taught me anything, it was that Ivy was it for me. I was never meant to be with Amber, not for the long run, because this wild redhead was supposed to be my endgame. I realized it when I watched my friends together and discovered that I watched Ivy with the look on my face that Zach wore whenever he looked at Rae.

"Thanks, butterfly," I said softly, the pads of my fingers pressing deeper into her hips. *Christ*, I wanted to kiss her.

She looked gorgeous today. Just like every day. She was

dressed for a rodeo in bootcut jeans that hugged her ass to perfection, and a burnt orange tee with the image of a cowboy riding a horse with a lasso above his head printed on the front. She'd been complaining about her tits for weeks, bitching about how much bigger they were getting, and damn if they didn't make my mouth water with the way they stretched out that shirt. Her boots were cute but functional, made for walking so her feet wouldn't end up aching by the end of the night. She could have been wearing a burlap sack and she still would have been the most gorgeous woman here.

"You hungry, sweetheart? I thought I might take you around to some of my favorite booths."

Her eyes rounded as she exclaimed, "Yes, I'm *starving*."

Lennix's mouth dropped open. "How is that possible? You've had a funnel cake, a bag of popcorn, a liter soda, and three fried Oreos all since we got here. Not to mention the turkey leg you were gnawing on like a freaking cavewoman."

I laughed as Ivy shot her friend a scowl. I'd noticed my woman's appetite had really picked up the past couple weeks. She'd gone from barely being able to keep anything down to eating me under the table. And what the hell did it say about me that I found the idea of watching her eat a whole damn turkey leg sexy?

She'd put back on the weight she lost from all those

weeks of being sick, but other than that—and her boobs, of course—her body still wasn't showing any outward changes. I found myself excited for the day when she finally started to show so I could finally see signs of my baby that she was carrying. I wanted to watch her belly expand as my baby grew inside her. Christ, just thinking about seeing her like that made me hard. Who the hell would have guessed that I'd have a breeding kink?

I cast Zach a silent look, my shoulders sagging with relief when he read what I was trying to communicate.

"It's getting late. I got a new gelding arriving at the ranch early tomorrow, so I think we're gonna hit the road."

I didn't miss the way Ivy's face fell, and it made me want to crow with victory. "Oh. Okay."

"You can ride home with me if you want to stick around a little longer," I told her. When I found out our crew was coming with her today to watch me ride, I'd ask Zach to make sure she didn't drive herself. First, because I'd recently discovered Ivy was a terrible driver. And second, because it would give me an hour alone with her on the ride back to Hope Valley.

As quickly as her face had fallen, she perked right back up. "Yeah, okay. Let's do it."

We bid goodbye to our friends, and once they took off,

I held my hand out to Ivy. "Come on, wild woman. Let's get you fed."

Walking through the rodeo grounds hand in hand with Ivy felt like we were on our first date. We'd had countless meals together in the past when I'd swing by the lodge on her lunch hour to take her for a picnic in the field of wildflowers she loved so much, but this was different. I felt like I got to show her off like this. I was proud to have her on my arm as we bounced from one carnival booth to another. I spent twenty bucks on a stupid game where I had to shoot a cheap water gun into a stupidly small hole to win her a stuffed pink unicorn she'd squealed over.

The thing was ugly as sin, but watching her carry it around, clutching it to her chest like her most prized possession, made warmth bloom in my chest. The way she'd smiled at me when I finally won the damn thing made me feel like the luckiest man on the planet. There wasn't anything I wouldn't do to make her smile like that every day.

I took her to some of my favorite food tents, loading up on anything she thought looked good, so by the time we sat down at an empty picnic table, we had a paper boat of loaded nachos, two corndogs slathered in mustard, chili cheese tots, sausage on a stick, street corn, and a caramel apple.

I let out a sigh of relief when we finally sat down. I would have been happy to walk laps all around the fairgrounds if it made her happy, but I'd tweaked my knee earlier when I jumped off that bull, and the damn thing was throbbing like a bitch. If I'd been smart, I would have headed home to ice it and pop a couple anti-inflammatories, but as long as Ivy was having a good time, I'd swallow down the pain.

She sat down on the bench across from me and popped a nacho into her mouth, chewing slowly as she studied me.

"What?" I asked with a small chuckle as I loaded my chip with jalapeño slices and tossed it into my mouth.

"How has your knee been doing since you hurt it last year?" Her tone was conversational, but I couldn't help but feel she was digging for something.

"It's fine," I said as I scraped a glob of mustard off one of the corndogs and bit into it, using our food to hide the fact her question had caught me off guard. "All better."

"Really?" She cocked her head to the side, her pretty blue eyes scrutinizing me from across the table. "Because it kind of looked like it was giving you a little trouble when you hit the ground earlier."

Fucking hell. Who knew the woman was so damn observant? I lifted the plastic cup of beer to my lips and drank deeply, giving myself a second to come to terms with the lie I was going to stick to. "It was nothing, just a little tender is all. I'm perfectly fine."

She worried her plump bottom lip between her teeth. "You sure?"

I reached across the table and took her hand in mine. The difference in size between her small, delicate hand and my large, rough one never failed to amaze me. "I'm sure," I told her. "You don't have to worry about me."

I meant it too. I knew my knee was fucked up, and that any doctor in their right mind would tell me I shouldn't be riding anymore, but I couldn't stop now. Not when I was so close to the World Championship. Not when I still had something to prove to the people who'd given up on me.

It was on that thought that a voice spoke up, taking the great evening I'd been having and flushing it right down the toilet.

"Well isn't this cozy."

Chapter Twenty-Four

IVY

The air around Connor changed in an instant. He went from calm and happy to tense and pissed, all from one blink to the next as he turned to look at the person who'd come up to our table. It was that bull rider from earlier, the cocky one with the Chicklet teeth, with the brunette latched onto his side, her left hand pressed to his chest to show off the sparkly rock on her ring finger, the woman whose tongue he'd been sucking on for all to see.

My attention bounced between the two men. There was no missing the animosity crackling in the air between the two of them as they stared each other down, but while they only had angry eyes for each other, the woman's focus pinned on me. She watched me with a combination of curiosity and disgust, like I'd done something to personally offend her.

"Move along, Grimes," Connor gritted out between clenched teeth, his fingers around mine tensing even tighter.

"Don't you want to introduce me to your friend?" He cast that toothpaste-commercial smile at me and extended his hand my way. "Vance Grimes. Pleasure to meet you, little lady."

My top lip curled away from my teeth at *little lady*. What a condescending prick. No wonder the woman pinned to him hadn't said a word yet. She was only a trophy. Something he touted around for show.

"Seriously?" I said under my breath. "I'm not your little lady."

"Get your fuckin' hand away from her before I snap it off," Connor growled.

"Whoa, no need to get hostile." The pretty boy let out a chortle and held up his hands in surrender like he meant no harm, though anyone with eyes could see plain as day that he'd come over to our table with the intention of starting shit. When he put his arms down, he tucked one hand into his pocket and placed the other right on the woman's ass cheek, giving it a firm squeeze and a light smack.

What the hell was with these two and the nauseating PDA?

"Just wanted to come over and congratulate you on a good ride, that's all."

The corners of Connor's mouth curled upward, his smile looking downright vicious. "You mean you came over to congratulate me for knocking you back to number two again?"

Oh shit. I had a feeling those were fighting words.

Pretty boy's eyes narrowed, and I could practically see the wheels moving behind his calculating gaze. "No, actually. I wanted to congratulate you on breakin' your dry spell. Looks like your appreciation for the buckle bunnies has finally returned."

Connor moved quickly, but so did I, anticipating what he was going to do before he could do it. He shot to his feet and surged toward the asshole in the too clean jeans and too crisp button-down. This prick had poser written all over him. The reason he came over to start shit was because he knew he would never be as good as Connor, and that left an awful, bitter taste in his mouth. As long as Connor was on the circuit, he'd always be number two.

I put myself in front of Connor before he could do something that could get him in trouble. Adopting a similar stance to Rodeo Barbie and bracing my hand against his chest, I plastered myself to his side to stop him from lunging.

"Don't," I whispered into his ear, feeling his heart beating wildly in his chest. "He's absolutely not worth it."

"Letting your women fight your battles now, Bennett?"

I turned to face this movie villain wannabe and snorted derisively, giving him a sweep with my eyes before making a face that told him how lacking I found him to be.

"No, I'm actually doing you a favor. I'm worried if he knocked those giant horse teeth down your throat you'd choke to death on them."

Connor made a choking sound of his own, and when I looked up at him I saw he'd lowered his head and curled his lips between his teeth to keep from laughing.

The asshole's cheeks started to turn red as snickers rose up from the tables around us, more people listening in as the tension between the two men became obvious.

"You're a mouthy little buckle bunny, aren't you? Do you even know who I am?"

"Not a buckle bunny," I said, pointing at my chest. "And I get that you're lowkey calling me a whore, but I'm too busy staring at those Chicklets you call teeth to pay much mind to your insults. And what kind of name is Vance anyway? What are you, some eighties high-school-movie douchebag?" I gave him my snarkiest smile. "You look the part with the ridiculous amount of gel you put in your hair. I bet you're dying to pop your collar right now, aren't you?"

"Oh shit," I heard someone mumble behind me as the giggles and laughter around us grew louder.

Connor's arm wrapped around my waist, squeezing me tighter to him, and a flutter worked through me at the feel of all his hard and strong pressed against my soft. My nipples stiffened and pressed insistently against the cups of my bra.

Rodeo Barbie scrunched her nose and curled her lip at me. "Wow, Con. You really scraped the bottom of the barrel with this one, didn't you?" She fluttered her lashes at the man standing beside me, and all the pieces suddenly clicked into place. He'd been with her. That's why she was keeping that gaudy ring front and center.

I'd never been a jealous woman, but I suddenly wanted to scratch this woman's eyes out and stake my claim on Connor for all to see. So I did it in the only way I could think.

I looked up at Connor from beneath my lashes, giving him a pouty look as I declared, "I'm bored with this, honey." Then I took his hand and placed it on my stomach in front of everyone. "And our chickpea's craving a churro. What do you say we get out of here?"

I didn't miss the gasp from the woman or the narrow-eyed look *Vance* shot to my belly, but I didn't spare either of them another look as I waited to see how Connor was going to play this situation I'd gotten us in.

When he leaned in and brushed his lips lightly against mine, my whole body lit up like a Christmas tree. My hormones went nuts and a voice in the back of my head started screaming at me to climb this man like a tree.

"Let's go, baby. It's gettin' late anyway. Should probably get you into bed soon."

I had to lock my knees to keep from melting at the way he lowered his voice on that last sentence, innuendo dripping from his words. Then I remembered that once we got home, Connor would go to the carriage house and I'd be climbing into bed by myself.

I popped one last chili cheese tot into my mouth before letting Connor lead me away with an arm securely wrapped around my waist. With one last glance over my shoulder, I called out, "So long, Number Two. Better luck next time."

"Christ, you're vicious when you want to be," Connor chuckled under his breath, and I couldn't help but preen at the respect in his tone.

"That guy pissed me off, coming over like that just to get under your skin."

"Aww." He pulled me tighter and lowered his lips to

press a kiss to the top of my head as we walked. "Were you defending my honor, butterfly?"

I was, because something had come over me in that moment that made me feel like Connor was mine to defend. It was a ridiculous notion, I knew. We were friends, nothing more. But my head, my heart, and my body suddenly weren't on the same page like they'd been for the past several weeks, and the thick, straight line I'd drawn between Connor and me was starting to look a little wonky.

I felt Connor's body tense up as his gait slowed, and when I tipped my head back to see what had caused the change in him, I saw that his focus was on an old man about fifteen yards in front of us.

The guy was the definition of old-school cowboy, from his boots to his broken-in cowboy hat to the gray, bushy handlebar mustache above his top lip. Whatever silent communication transpired between the two men with little more than a look left the air chilled. Then the old man shook his head and made a face of disappointment before turning his back on Connor and walking away, dismissing him without even saying a word.

The teasing Connor from seconds ago was gone, shadows now blocking out the light and humor that had been in his eyes earlier. This was a version of Connor I'd only seen once before. When I told him I could raise our baby without him. His frame sagged with defeat, and seeing him like that broke my heart.

"Who was that?" I asked quietly.

He heaved out a sigh, his arm falling from around me as he brought the other up to scrub at the stubble covering his jaw. I immediately missed the heat of his touch, my heart sinking at the distance he put between us. He didn't say a word as we left the fairgrounds and wound our way through the sea of cars and trucks to his.

He didn't say anything until he helped me into the passenger seat and rounded the hood, climbing in on his side. He started the engine and placed his hand on the gearshift like he was about to put the truck in reverse, but instead of doing that, he spoke. "His name's Dusty Silver." Christ, the guy even had a cowboy name.

I twisted in my seat to face him better, but he kept his eyes pointed at something beyond the windshield, something he wasn't seeing, given that he was lost in a memory.

"He's a legend," he continued, his voice void of all emotion. "One of the best bull riders of his time. He used to be my mentor. He trained me, taught me everything I know. He was like family to me."

Sadness filled my chest. "*Was* like family?"

Connor blinked, finally turning his head in my direction, and what I saw in his gaze tore my heart to shreds. "Turned out, while I was looking up to him like a second father, he was thinking about how I could further his reputation. Had a couple bad rides some time back and got in my own head about it. When that happens, your rides start to suffer. I hit a patch of bad luck, dropped in standing, so Dusty dropped me," he said with a shrug. "Scraped me off for a bull rider he thought could carry him further."

"Vance."

He nodded, and I suddenly hated the guy even more than I already had. "Now I'm starting to think I should have let you knock those ridiculous teeth out."

His laugh didn't hold any humor, his smile brittle. "That happened right around the same time I caught my fiancée cheating on me with that same *fuckin'* guy."

And the hits just kept on coming. I sucked in a sharp, pained gasp. "You were engaged to Rodeo Barbie?"

He nodded, knowing who I was referring to. "It was years ago, and I now know it never would have worked because what I thought was love really wasn't. But losing two people I cared about at the same time, being tossed over by both of them . . . it fucked with my head for a really long time."

In that moment, everything clicked into place. Why Connor had gone from hot to cold all those months ago. Why we shared what I thought had been a special night—one of the best nights of my life—only to wake up and find him gone. It made sense now, and as much as it broke my heart, it pissed me off even more that two people who were supposed to care about him, who were supposed to have his back, had dismissed him so easily.

"I'm so sorry," I whispered, reaching over to wrap my fingers around his thick, corded forearm.

He shrugged and slid the gearshift in reverse. "It's over now. No point in dwelling on it anymore. Let's put this night behind us, yeah?"

I nodded, giving him a smile that I hoped didn't look as sad as I felt, because I didn't want to put the night behind us. Not the whole thing anyway.

Because the truth was, before those assholes had showed up to ruin it, it had been one of the best nights I'd had in a really long time.

I stood at the window of my office, looking in the direction of the barn where I knew Connor was working for the day. I chewed anxiously on my thumbnail as a million thoughts raced through my head.

After that brief run-in with that Dusty guy the night before, the Connor who I'd spent the evening laughing and stuffing my face with, the Connor who had managed to rev me up with every look and touch, never made another appearance.

I'd toyed with the idea of inviting him in for a drink the whole hour-long drive back to Hope Valley, but as soon as he walked me to my back door, he'd issued a curt "goodnight" and disappeared into the carriage house.

I went into my own house and got ready for bed, alone and bereft, surprised I was missing him. When I finally fell asleep, my dreams were full of Connor. Touching me and teasing me the way he was so good at doing. Tasting me.

I woke up with an ache in my core that refused to go away. I'd tried touching myself, even whipping out my vibrator. I got off, but it was barely enough to take the edge off. I felt like I was coming out of my skin, like I was going to lose my mind if I didn't get some relief.

And there was only one person I wanted.

I couldn't deny it anymore. I craved him. I wanted him. I *needed* him.

Before I knew what was happening, I was driving a UTV toward the barn in search of Connor. He wasn't inside, so I headed toward the pen, stopping briefly to say hi to Gretel. I found out not too long ago that she was pregnant as well, but while I had yet to pop, she was swelling bigger every day.

She let out an unhappy bleat as I patted her head like she was lamenting the pains of pregnancy. "You and me both, sister."

With one last rub to her head, I headed for the round pen where Connor was working that same black horse he'd been in there with the last time I was here. I braced my forearms on the railing and rested my chin on top as I watched him work, pulling my bottom lip between my teeth and biting down to keep from moaning.

He was so goddamn sexy. So sure and confident in

what he was doing despite the size and weight the animal had on him. Not only did his confidence turn me on, but so did the gentle way he handled the filly. The low, soothing tone, the words of encouragement and praise. It took me back to our night in the barn and how he kept calling me a good girl, praising me for how well I took his cock.

God, I wanted that again.

I'd gotten his attention at some point, but I was too lost in memory to notice him moving in my direction. A shame, really, because I loved watching that man move.

"Hey, butterfly. Surprised to see you down here."

I licked my lips, suddenly feeling nervous. "H-hi."

He quirked a brow, his eyes growing concerned. "Everything good?"

I nodded a bit too quickly. "Yeah. It's fine. It's just . . . do you have a few minutes to talk?" Or to strip me bare and fuck me like it was what you were built to do.

He pushed back a step, his eyes searching my face for a few beats. "Sure. Just give me a sec. I can get one of the other guys to take over here."

My nod was much calmer that time, and a second later, he was moving toward the horse, a sharp whistle shooting in the direction of a few of the cowboys who had been sitting on the fence watching Connor work the horse. He waved one of them over, giving the guy instructions I couldn't hear before nodding his head, and started toward the gate. He caught my eye and jerked his chin, silently telling me to follow him.

I did, trailing a few steps behind as he led us into the large tack room. He held the door open, waiting for me to enter before closing it behind me.

I took a moment to take everything in, the buckets of brushes, the bridles hanging from hooks on the walls, the rows of saddles, all cleaned and conditioned, waiting for use. It smelled like leather and dust.

"You sure everything's okay?" he asked again. I dragged my attention to him as he pulled the work gloves off his hands and stuffed them into his back pocket. He braced his hands on his trim hips, giving me his full attention.

"You didn't come by this morning." His brows winged up, befuddlement etched into his expression. I started to ramble, unable to stop myself. "I mean, not that I *expected* you to or anything. It's just . . . you usually come by the house in the mornings before you head out here. And you didn't this morning. And after last night . . ." I strummed my teeth against my bottom lip nervously. "I worried that maybe you weren't okay. After seeing . . . you know who." Christ, I was talking about them like they were Lord Voldemort. "I just wanted to make sure *you* were okay. Since I didn't see you this morning."

He blinked, then a moment later his features cleared of

confusion and a sultry, dimpled smile stretched across his face, making my clit pulse.

"Butterfly, did you miss me this mornin'?"

Well, here goes nothing, I thought as I ran my hands down the front of my light gray pencil skirt. "Yes."

He rocked back, my honesty slamming into him and causing his eyes to widen before the silky chocolate brown darkened and his jaw clenched. His throat worked on a swallow. "Say it again."

I licked my dry lips and looked down at my hands. "I missed you," I said so softly I was sure he barely heard me.

I hadn't even heard him move across the room when he was suddenly in front of me, his fingers pressing beneath my chin, forcing my face up to his. His voice was deep and gravelly as he asked, "You want me right now, baby? Is that what this is about?"

God, I did. I wanted him so damn bad. "Yes," I said on a breathy sigh.

A low, craggy sound worked its way up his throat and broke free right before he dove in, slamming his lips against mine and trapping my yelp of surprise inside my mouth. With one swipe of his tongue, I opened for him, moaning as his tongue dove in and brushed against my own.

"Jesus, Ivy. Do you have any goddamn clue how badly I've wanted you?" He fisted the hair at the nape of my neck and pulled my head back, exposing my throat and dragging his tongue along my sensitive flesh. "Fucking *months*," he hissed as one hand wrapped around to grip my ass and the other traveled up my chest. "Since the last time I had you. I wasn't nearly done with you when you ran off on me."

"Connor." That one word came out in a throaty plea.

"Can't tell you the number of times I've beat off to the thought of you." I moaned, wanting him to tell me everything. "All alone in that carriage house, strokin' my dick and wishin' it was you on your knees in front of me, your plump little lips stretched around my cock. He brought his hand to my mouth, dragging the pad of his thumb across my lips before sliding it past. I closed around it, giving it a suck that made him rumble a sound like a purring lion.

"Tell me what you need," he commanded, the playful side of him giving way to the dominant man who knew how to manipulate my body better than anyone else ever had.

"You," I whimpered, lifting up on my toes to get at his mouth. "I need you. Right now." He brought his hand to my breast, cupping it through my top and dragging his damp thumb across my aching nipple.

I let out a cry loud enough it caused him to jerk back. "You okay? Did I hurt you?

"No," I panted, a new flood of arousal soaking my panties. "They're just so sensitive."

That statement set something off in him, and before I knew it, he had me stripped down to nothing but my heels. His eyes were molten as he cupped my breast and lifted it, watching my face as he lowered his own and sucked my nipple between his lips.

I yelped, my hands shooting up to grip his hair in tight fists as the sensation of his mouth sucking on my breast shot straight to my clit. "Oh God. Connor." I whimpered as bolts of lightning shot off between my thighs. He switched between nipples, laving and sucking and nipping with his teeth until I was writhing uncontrollably. I'd never felt anything like this before. My core clenched over and over until my release slammed into me unexpectedly. With only his mouth on my tits, he pushed me over the edge into a climax that made my knees buckle.

I would have gone down if he hadn't wrapped his arms around my waist and kept me standing. He looked at me with wide-eyed wonder. "Did you just . . .?"

I chewed on the corner of my mouth and nodded. "More," I demanded breathily, reaching between us and cupping his straining dick trapped beneath his pants. "Give me this. I want this fat cock inside me right now."

"Jesus, fuck," he grunted, jerking his hips harder into my hand.

"I want you to stretch me wide open. No preparing my pussy or getting me ready for you."

He took two steps back, that dominant, alpha cowboy standing before me now as he reached behind his neck and whipped his shirt off. His belt buckle clinked as he undid it, and I watched in rapt fascination as he popped the button, lowered the zipper, and reached in to pull his thick, rigid cock free.

"This what you want?" he asked as he stroked his hand upward, gathering the pre-cum at its tip and using it to slick his hand back down.

I stood completely and unabashedly naked before him and nodded.

"Then do as I say. Get down on your knees."

I lowered as gracefully as I could, so turned on I didn't even register the harsh concrete floor abrading my skin. He must have realized then how unforgiving the ground was, because he clucked his tongue and shook his head. "No, that won't do, baby."

I tracked his every step as he moved around the room. First he grabbed a horse blanket from the rack against the back wall. Then he moved over to a hook near the door that had ropes draped across it. He fingered each one like he was testing the fibers before nodding to himself decisively and unlooping one of the ropes.

I swallowed down the thick lump of lust that had formed in my throat. "What's that for?"

He winked and my clit tingled. "You'll see. Now put this under your knees."

I took the blanket and placed it on the ground, the softness a massive improvement as I kneeled on it.

He came to stand in front of me, his cock still protruding from his jeans and making my mouth water. "Hands," he commanded on a grunt.

I lifted my wrists, unsure what was about to happen, but trusting him enough to go with it without worry. I sucked in a breath as he whipped the surprisingly soft rope around my wrists, binding them together in an intricate knot I wouldn't be able to get out of no matter how hard I tried. He took the long length that he'd left free and stretched it up above my head, creating another impressive knot that fingers the size of his shouldn't have been able to make with such ease, then he looped it around a hook high on the wall.

"What—" I gave my wrists a testing jerk, the knots holding strong.

Connor walked around me, coming to stand in front of me and running a gentle hand down my hair. "You trust me, butterfly?"

I swallowed and gave him a nod. "Y-yes."

"Good girl." And there it was, that praise that had my pussy weeping.

He moved behind me, and I heard the shuffling of his

boots and the clinking of his belt as he shoved his jeans lower. I didn't look back to see what he was doing, but I felt the heat of his body at my back just before his hand slid down my ribs and caressed my right hip. "Lean forward a bit, baby. Just enough to pull the rope tight. I won't let you fall."

I did as he instructed, my heart hammering inside my chest as I hinged forward at the waist. My arms stayed stretched above my head, catching me mid-lead so my chest was nearly parallel with the floor. It was a position that wouldn't take long to start to hurt, but before I could worry, Connor looped my hair around his fist and used it to pull my head back, holding me stationary and taking some of the pressure off my arms. He was using my hair like the reins for a horse. It felt dirty and depraved and I was so fucking turned on thinking about what we looked like.

I could feel my arousal dripping down my inner thighs, and I knew I was so worked up that he was going to be able to slide inside me easily.

He notched the head of his cock into place, nudging the first half-inch inside me. "You ready to be fucked hard and raw, baby?"

"Please, Connor," I begged. "Do it now."

His hips bucked forward and he drove himself inside me to the hilt, letting out a string of curses as I cried at the invasion, the pain barely registering before it gave way to pleasure so intense I couldn't breathe. He stretched me so perfectly, better than any other man had before.

"Fuck yeah," he grunted as he began riding me hard, those magical hips of his moving against me like they did when he was up on that bull. "Fuck, if you could see how well your pussy's stretching for me right now." He pounded into me, grunting with each forward thrust into my tight heat.

I could already feel another release building, this one threatening to be absolutely devastating. "Christ, you're such a good girl, letting me tie you up like this and fuck you hard."

"Don't stop," I pleaded, gasping for breath as the pressure inside me built. "Please, don't stop Connor. I'm close."

"So goddamn perfect for me," he growled, his fist tightening in my hair. I twisted my hands and gripped the length of rope, desperately needing something to hold on to. "You gonna take my cum, baby? You gonna beg me for it while I fill you up?"

"Yes, please!" I cried. "I need it. Give it to me."

"You first," he gritted out. Then he brought the hand that had been gripping my hip up and brought it down on my ass with a loud crack. The searing pain of his hand slapping my ass hard enough to leave a mark was all I needed to explode. A million nuclear missiles detonated inside me. I started to scream so loud Connor had to lean over my back and clamp his hand over my mouth to muffle the noises I couldn't possibly control on my own.

"Fuck, your pussy's grippin' me so goddamn hard, I can't. Can't hold back."

I clenched myself around him, forcing him to let go and join me. We came together in the middle of the tack room, my own climax so intense I swore there were a few seconds when I blacked out.

"Fuck," he gasped, bending over my back and pressing kisses to my shoulder as he worked the knot and loosened the rope around my wrists. His arm banded around my waist before I could faceplant on the floor, lifting me so my back was flush with his chest. His dick continued to jerk inside me, the hot ropes of cum coating my walls as his lips dragged along my skin. "*Fuck*, Ivy. I've missed you, baby."

All I could think was that I had missed him too. Terribly. And that was a huge problem.

Chapter Twenty-Six

IVY

The paper sheet beneath me crinkled as I sat on the bed in Dr. Shaundry's office, swinging my legs back and forth as I tried to settle my nerves. I couldn't shake the feeling that something wasn't right, and I didn't mean the ridiculous paper gown that was supposed to somehow protect my modesty when my ass was literally hanging out in the breeze.

Today marked seventeen weeks. I was into my second trimester, and had the tiniest little pooch to show the growing baby in my belly. Most of the time it looked like I'd eaten a giant burrito, but I knew what the little bump was. Nearly the instant it popped, Connor had become obsessed.

He was constantly touching my belly, caressing it lovingly, placing a kiss every chance he could, or leaning down to talk softly to our chickpea. Now that he finally had a visual representation of what we had created, he couldn't seem to get enough.

He couldn't seem to get enough of me either, and the feeling was more than mutual.

That was the problem. That afternoon in the tack room had flipped a switch. We were going at it every chance we got. I couldn't seem to get enough of him. Every time I thought I might finally be sated, he'd do or say something that would get my engine going all over again. I told myself over and over it was pregnancy hormones driving me crazy, but deep down, I knew better. It was him.

He was the man I'd fallen for when he first came to Hope Valley all those long months ago. The man I couldn't help but confide in. The man I wanted to know everything about. And that terrified me. I tried to keep the things between us as straightforward as possible. We were friends. We were going to be co-parents. We just happened to like ripping each other's clothes off and going at it until neither of us could walk. It didn't mean feelings had to get involved.

Only, no matter how many times I told myself that, I'd find myself tangled up in those pesky little feelings all over again. I was so tangled up with Connor I wasn't sure

where he ended and I began. I could play aloof all I
wanted, but inside, I was a wreck.

He'd stomped my heart to smithereens the first time,
and I was recklessly opening myself up to that again, only I
wasn't the only one who would suffer if he freaked out
again.

It wasn't just my heart I had to protect this time
around.

A knock sounded on the door, pulling me from my
thoughts right before the doctor poked her head inside.
"Momma Young," she greeted with a smile that instantly
put me at ease.

"Hi."

She looked around the room as she moved to the sink
and washed her hands. "No Daddy today?"

"No. He had to go out of town for work." That was
what felt so off about the appointment. Connor wasn't
there. He wanted to be. He was actually really upset about
missing it, but I assured him it would be okay. There
would be other appointments that wouldn't fall on the
same day as a big rodeo. He was in Tennessee right now
and wouldn't be home until later tonight. I tried to
reschedule for another day, but Dr. Shaundry was apparently the most sought-after OB in the area, and this was
the closest appointment I could get.

It was his job, and it required traveling, even with

Hope Valley being his new hometown. I understood that. I just . . . missed him.

"That's okay. Happens all the time, believe me. We'll take plenty of pictures for him to look at once he gets back."

She instructed me to lie back on the reclined bed. Now that I was in my second trimester, she didn't have to use that creepy, uncomfortable wand. She squeezed a dollop of jelly onto my stomach and placed the transducer against my belly. She slid the controller around for a few seconds before the room filled with the sound of that lovely heartbeat. "Ah, there's baby."

My heart squelched as I watched the monitor, seeing the perfect little profile of my baby. I could see the forehead and the nose. As I watched, I could have sworn I saw it lift its tiny little hand to pop its thumb into its mouth.

She let out a little laugh as she started clicking buttons near the monitor, taking picture after picture that I couldn't wait to share with Connor. "Oh, wow. Looks like it wants to show off today."

"What do you mean?" She tilted the device and squinted at the monitor. "Well, most of the time I'd wait to try and tell the gender, but your little one has decided to make it known. If you want, I can tell you what you're having."

I looked to the screen, trying to see what she was

seeing, but it was just a bunch of floating clouds. "Right now?" I asked in amazement. "You can really see it?"

"Yep." Her smile grew. "Right now. Your baby is *not* being shy, that's for sure."

I let out a little giggle. "That's from its father's side." I wanted to know so badly, but not having Connor here was holding me back. This was something I wanted to share with him. I didn't want to find out what we were having without him.

"Do you think you could write it down and put it in an envelope? That way we can open it together tonight."

"Absolutely." She tucked the transducer away and wiped my bump clean before helping me sit up straight. "Why don't you go ahead and get dressed? I'll take care of that for you and print those pictures for Dad."

By the time I left the office I was downright giddy. I couldn't *wait* for Connor to get home.

I WAS SOAKING IN THE BATHTUB, USING THE warm water to ease some of the round ligament pain that decided to creep up on me when I heard Connor's truck drive up. A smile pulled at my face as I pulled the plug to drain the tub and climbed out. I quickly dried off and scurried to my room to get dressed, throwing on a pair of cotton lounge shorts and a matching cropped hoody.

I expected to find Connor in the living room or kitchen when I came down the stairs. Since we started sleeping together he spent most of his time in the main house with me. He curled up on the couch with me every evening to relax in front of the TV, and when I inevitably fell asleep, he carried me upstairs to bed and crawled in with me. Other than his trip out of town, we hadn't slept in different beds in weeks. I figured he'd come right here, but as I rounded the landing, the house was quiet.

"Con, you home?" I called, looking out at the window that overlooked the driveway to see if he was still in his truck. I didn't stop to consider if he went to the carriage house first. I knew from our phone call earlier he'd come in first place again, so it wasn't like he was in a bad mood or something and wanted to lick his wounds in private.

I moved into the kitchen, noticing the lights were on in the carriage house. Excitement was still fizzing in my veins when I snatched the envelope off the counter and bolted out the back door, practically skipping down the stone path that cut through the garden and led to the carriage house.

I rapped my knuckles against the wood quickly but didn't wait for a response before barging in. "Connor, you aren't gonna believe—" The words died on my tongue when I saw him stretched out in the reclining chair in the living room, dressed in nothing but tight black boxer briefs. That would usually have been enough to stop me in my tracks, but it wasn't the distinct bulge behind the cotton that had my attention this time.

"Oh my, God! What happened?" I rushed to him and dropped down to the floor beside the chair.

"It's fine," he said, but I saw the clench in his jaw and the tense lines around his eyes as he said it. He was in pain. "I just need to ice it, is all. It'll be good as new in a couple days."

My jaw dropped as I looked at the knee he was referring to. "Connor, that's . . . there's no way in hell your knee will be good as new in a couple days. It's the size of a grapefruit!"

The damn thing was swollen to twice its normal size, the skin around it bright red and angry. It looked like it was agonizing.

"It does this from time to time. Just need to get the swelling down, and it'll be good to go for the next rodeo in Hampton in a couple weeks."

I sputtered, my gaze darting behind his obviously *seriously* injured knee and his face to see if he was joking. He had to be joking. He couldn't possibly think it was okay to climb on the back of a bull in the condition he was in.

I closed my eyes and took a few calming breaths so I

didn't lose my shit completely. "Connor, you can't ride in a couple weeks. This looks really serious. You're going to hurt yourself."

The muscle in his jaw ticked and his eyes went flinty. "See, that's why I came here first. I knew you were gonna make a big deal out of nothin'."

I shot to my feet and jabbed my finger toward his knee. "*That* is not nothing! And of course I'm making a big deal out of it. You ride another bull with your knee in this condition, you're going to seriously hurt yourself. Or worse!"

It was the *or worse* that had my stomach bottoming out. "Connor, please." I tried a different tactic since yelling and arguing wasn't getting me anywhere. "Please, be reasonable, okay? You have two weeks before the rodeo in Hampton. Can't you try and get in to see a doctor before then? Maybe they can give you something to help."

He shoved up in the chair like he wanted to storm out of it and start pacing, only he couldn't, because his knee was *completely fucked up*!

"I can't go to a doctor, Ivy," he clipped at me, using a tone he'd never used with me before. "If I go to a doctor, he'll tell me I can't ride."

I threw my hands out at my sides, shrieking, "Then don't ride!"

"I have to!" he shouted back. "Fuck!" He reached up

and dragged a hand down his face, and I noticed the exhaustion there for the first time. "I have to, okay? I don't expect you to understand, but this is all I am. I'm a bull rider. That's it."

I crouched down and reached for his hand, but he snatched it away before I could grab it. "That's not true," I said gently. "Connor, you're so much more than a bull rider. It isn't who you are. It's what you do."

"I have to ride," he gritted out, his jaw working back and forth.

"Why?" I stood tall, frustration warring with concern. "What could possibly be so important that you'd put your own safety at risk?"

"I have to show them they were wrong about me." All the air expelled from my lungs on a single exhale. "I have to prove to them that I'm better than what they thought. That I'm the best." He raked his hands through his hair in frustration. "I can't quit now. When I go out, I have to go out on top."

I stood frozen, trying to understand the pain in his heart that would drive him to do something so reckless, just to prove himself to people who didn't deserve a second of his time.

"Is that the only reason you're riding? To stick it to a few miserable people whose opinions shouldn't matter?"

"They matter to me," he grumbled, and I felt a piece of my heart break off.

I sniffled, giving my head a shake. I could feel the tears coming, but I refused to let them fall until I was in the privacy of my own home. "Then I feel sorry for you," I whispered, placing a hand on my belly. "Because you're so wrapped up in the past that you're putting them before all the good you have in your life *now*."

With that, I placed the envelope on the table beside his chair and turned to leave.

"What's this?"

With my hand on the knob, I cast a look at him over my shoulder. "It's the baby's gender. The doctor was able to tell at the appointment today. I was so excited I had her write it down and seal it so we could open it and find out what we're having together. Because while you were out there hurting yourself"—I pointed at the envelope—"that's what mattered to *me*."

With that, I walked out of the carriage house and closed the door behind me.

The tingle at the base of my spine was building. I could feel my balls getting tight, but I couldn't bring myself to let go.

This wasn't right.

I never thought I'd describe sex with Ivy as wrong, but that was what this felt like. *Wrong*. She was riding me. I was wedged as deep inside her as I could be, but she was disconnected.

"Butterfly, slow down." She kept the same pace, her head tossed back and her eyes squeezed closed. Her hands were braced on my chest, her nails digging into my skin there, but in that moment, I was only a dick she was using to get off. She was shutting herself off from me. She'd been doing that for nearly two weeks now, ever since the fight in the carriage house.

Things had been strained since that night, and I knew I was at fault, but I didn't know how the fuck to fix it.

No, that wasn't right. I knew how.

I couldn't bring myself to give her what she'd asked for. What she had pleaded for as worry filled those deep blue eyes. Guilt had been eating away at me for two fucking weeks. It was why that envelope was still sitting in the carriage house, unopened.

A growl rumbled up from my chest as her pussy fluttered around me. "Look at me, baby."

She was shutting me out. It was a truth both of us had been ignoring since the fight, one we'd been tiptoeing around but refusing to acknowledge. We still slept together every night. We still fucked like the world's survival depended on it. But where it used to fill me up, it now felt empty. I got the feeling this was her way of trying to work me out from under her skin. I couldn't let that happen.

"Ivy, goddamn it. *Look at me*," I snapped.

When she kept those eyes from me. I couldn't take it any longer. Grabbing hold of her hips, I flipped us over so fast she let out a yelp. I drove back into her so hard her eyes widened, *finally* meeting mine.

"There you are," I breathed as I started fucking her hard and fast, driving both of us to the brink. "You aren't getting rid of me that easy, baby." I lowered my forehead to hers, kissing her with every ounce of love I felt for her. "I won't let you work me out."

I pulled back in time to see a single tear slide down her cheek right before her cunt clamped down around me and she screamed out my name with her release. I followed right after her, shooting deep inside her on a groan so deep it rattled my bones.

Once she'd wrung every drop from me, I collapsed on top of her, burying my face in the crook of her neck as I pleaded. "Don't take yourself from me, butterfly. I'm beggin' you." She sniffled and I felt the dampness from more tears. "Christ, please don't cry. You're killin' me."

She sniffled, shaking her head, sadness infused in every inch of her face. "I don't know if I can keep doing this," she whispered, slicing me right to the bone.

I brushed the tip of my nose against her. "You have to. Because I can't live without you." My throat felt like it was on fire as I held back my own tears. "I love you, Ivy. I'm so in love with you. You and this baby are my whole world."

Those blue eyes went wide, her swollen lips parting on a gasp. For one moment, she smiled up at me with such beauty, I could see and feel her love for me in return. Then she cupped my cheek and whispered, "Then don't ride this weekend. I'm begging you, Connor. I can't stand the thought of something happening to you."

My heart sank. Squeezing my eyes closed, I croaked, "I have to."

She pushed on my shoulder, and as badly as I wanted to stay right where I was, I rolled off her. She pushed up to sitting and scooted to the edge of the bed, clutching the sheet to her chest. She wouldn't look at me as she whispered, "If you feel that strongly, I don't think you should wait to leave. You should go now."

She got up and walked into the bathroom, closing the door behind her and throwing the lock.

Ivy

I felt like a zombie as I moved through the aisles of Fresh Foods, the local grocery store. The wheels on the cart rattled as I pushed it. My hands reached out and blindly grabbed things off the shelves, dropping them into the cart without even seeing what they were.

When I'd gotten out of the bathroom the night before, Connor hadn't been there. He'd done as I suggested and left. Not back to the carriage house. He'd *left*. Making the drive to the rodeo in Hampton.

I spent the rest of the night curled up in bed, clutching my little chickpea and crying my eyes out.

He was only a few hours away, but to me, it felt like he was in a whole other galaxy. Between the sadness and the worry, I felt sick to my stomach. The only reason I'd dragged myself out of my house and to the grocery store was because I couldn't stand the silence any longer.

Rae and Lennix had been texting regularly, but I couldn't bring myself to reply. Apparently Connor had texted Zach the night before and explained things. I wasn't sure what that meant or what he'd told him, but he made Zach promise that he and the girls would check on me while he was gone.

That broke my heart even more.

Snatching a bottle of alfredo sauce off a shelf, I tossed it into my cart, not caring in the slightest that I didn't *like* alfredo sauce. I rounded the corner and slammed my cart into someone else's.

"Oh God, I'm so sorry," I started. "I wasn't looking where I was going."

"That makes two of us."

My eyes came up and landed on Blythe. "Oh, hi."

She gave me a small smile that didn't reach her eyes. "Hi back."

I gripped the handle of my cart and shifted from foot

to foot. "Again, I'm really sorry for crashing into you. Guess I'm as bad at cart pushing as I am at driving."

"It's all good," she said with a tiny chuckle. Her smile faded as she scanned my face. "Are you okay?"

I was sure I looked a wreck. Not that I'd bothered to check a mirror before I left the house earlier. "Oh, yeah. I'm fine." I sniffled and brushed at my cheeks. "Just stupid boy stuff." I tried to play it off with a small laugh that fell flat.

She cocked her head to the side. "I'm guessing the stupid boy in question is the one who came with you to your first doctor's appointment?"

I nodded, sniffling again as my eyes began to water. "Yeah," I croaked, no longer caring if I had a breakdown in the middle of the grocery store. "Things are . . . complicated at the moment."

Sympathy washed over her features. "Do you love him?"

I nodded silently as the tears began to fall.

"Then can I make a suggestion?"

"Please." I was willing to hear anything at this point.

"Uncomplicate it," she said firmly. "Whatever the issue is, if you love him, do not stop until you find a way to make it work." She reached over and placed her hand on top of mine. "Believe me, your life can change in the blink of an eye, and when that happens, you won't even remember the complications. You'll only remember the things you miss."

With one last squeeze, she released my hand, untangled our carts, and kept going in the direction she'd been heading.

I stood rooted in place for what felt like an eternity before what she said finally sank in. Ditching my cart right where I'd been standing, I spun around and jogged out of the store, pulling my phone out of my purse and dialing as I ran to my car.

"Ivy?" Rae answered halfway through the first ring. "Are you okay?"

"I will be. You guys feel like going to a rodeo with me tonight so I can tell the father of my baby that I'm in love with him?"

She answered by shrieking through the line.

What the fuck am I doing?

The din of voices around me faded into nothing more than background noise as I sat in the changing room waiting for my number to be called. I couldn't even remember how I'd gotten here. My brain had shut down after Ivy walked away from me last night, and I'd been running on autopilot ever since.

All I could think about was the sadness in her eyes. All I could hear was her quiet, worried voice pleading with me. She was scared. For me.

She didn't give a shit if I was the best bull rider on the circuit. She didn't care what my name garnered in this world. All she cared about was my well-being. My safety. That was it.

"Is that the only reason you're riding? To stick it to a few miserable people whose opinions shouldn't matter?"

She was the only person to ever ask me why I was still doing this. The only one to care *why.* And looking back on my reasons now . . . they weren't good enough. I didn't love riding anymore. Not like I used to. And it wasn't because of Dusty or Amber or that fuckface Vance Grimes. I'd just outgrown it. I was older. I wanted different things. I looked at what Zach had with Rae, and I wanted that more than I wanted some belt buckle.

Reaching beneath the padded vest I was wearing, I pulled out the envelope I still hadn't opened, the one that held my future with Ivy.

When I died, I couldn't take any of that shit with me. But I could damn sure carry Ivy's love with me into the great beyond. I could take the memories of the family we built together. Ivy had been right. *Those* were the things that mattered. Not the opinions of a few miserable assholes and an arena full of strangers.

So what *the fuck* was I still doing here?

I shot up from the bench, ready to run the hell out of there, when the kid I'd helped several weeks back stepped in front of me, tugging nervously at his collar.

"Uh, Mr. Bennett."

"Just Connor. No need for the mister stuff."

He nodded, his Adam's apple working on a swallow. "Connor. I just wanted to thank you. You know, for helping me out a few weeks back? That tip you gave me about opening my hips up really helped. I've been sure to do that every ride since, and I think I'm getting better."

I stared at the kid standing in front of me, looking up at me the same way I imagined I'd looked up at Dusty Silver when I was his age. And the most miraculous thing happened in that moment. I realized I enjoyed helping that kid get better more than I actually did riding.

I never stopped to consider I could be some young kid's mentor, that I could pass down my knowledge to help someone else. I could do that. And I'd do it a hell of a lot better than Dusty did, because I wouldn't give a shit about my own reputation.

"I'm happy to help." I clapped him on the shoulder. "You've got real talent. You just need a little direction. If you ever find yourself in Hope Valley, look me up. I'd be happy to help you out some more."

His eyes bugged out like I'd just offered him my championship buckle. "Really? You'd do that?"

I chuckled. "There's no point in bein' the best if there's no real competition, kid. You want to make sure the guys you're goin' up against know their shit. That way, when you beat them, you know you earned it."

"Yeah," he breathed, his excitement growing as he nodded. "Okay! I'll be sure to do that. Hope Valley, you said?"

"Yep. It's where my family is. You're welcome any time. But when you show up, be prepared to work, because I'm not gonna go easy on you."

"You got it, mister—I mean Connor."

I gave him one more pat and started out of the changing room, calling back. "Good luck out there."

"Wait, where are you goin'!"

I beamed at the kid over my shoulder. "You're the first to hear it, but I'm officially retired!" I called back as I picked up the pace. The drive to Hope Valley was three hours. If I broke the speed limit, ran every stop sign and red light, and didn't get pulled over by the cops, I figured I could make it back home in two.

Home.

I was just about at the mouth of the hall when that shit-bag Vance stepped in front of me. I could tell by the cocky smirk on his punchable face he was looking to start some shit. Unfortunately for him, I was done. He wasn't even on my radar anymore.

"Congrats, man. You're officially number one," I said without stopping, calling back. "Not that you'll enjoy it, because you'll still be comparing yourself to me while I'll be too busy enjoyin' my life to even remember your name."

Fuck, that felt good to say.

I stepped out into the sunshine, ready to put on a burst of speed and run my ass all the way back to the parking lot. Knee be damned. I'd take this one last risk, then I'd go to the fucking doctor for Ivy and get it fixed.

Only my plan was delayed when I heard the sweetest, sexiest voice asking, "Can you tell me where I can find Connor Bennett?"

I rounded the corner and saw all that wild rose-gold hair shining in the sun. "Ivy?"

She whipped around, her lips stretching into a smile the moment her eyes landed on me. Then she shocked the hell out of me by taking a running leap and launching herself at me, wrapping her arms around my neck and sealing her lips against mine.

I fisted the hair at the back of her head and took the kiss deeper, drinking from her mouth. When the need for oxygen forced us apart, I rested my forehead against hers and breathed deeply, filling my lungs with lemon and basil to prove that she was really standing before me, wrapped in my arms.

"What are you doing here?"

She smiled up at me, love shining brightly in her eyes. "I came to cheer on my baby daddy."

I rocked back in shock. "What?"

She pulled in a fortifying breath and braced her hands on my chest, staring up at me earnestly as she said, "If this is what you want, I'm here. I have your back. No matter what happens, I'll always be wherever you are. That's what you do for the person you love, right?"

It took everything in me to keep from collapsing down on the dirt at hearing her say she loved me.

I took her mouth in a bruising kiss. "Say it, butterfly. I want to hear you say it."

"I love you, Connor. It's you and me and our little chickpea." She took my hand and pressed it against the tiny bump that had formed there almost overnight. I hadn't thought it was possible for her to get any sexier than she already was. Then I saw her belly swelling with my kid and that breeding kink was fully unlocked.

She didn't know it yet, but I fully intended to keep her pregnant with my babies for as long as I could get away with it.

"Christ, I fuckin' love you so much."

"I love you too," she repeated against my lips. "But . . ." She pulled back and looked around. "What are you doing out here? Should you be back getting ready?"

My dimples popped as I shook my head. "Nope. You can consider me officially retired. I'm goin' out on top."

Her lips parted on a gasp. "What?"

"I'm done, butterfly. Hal's been talkin' about retiring. Says he's too old to be a ranch foreman and wants to enjoy his last years fishin' and drinkin' beer. I was thinkin' that I'd talk to Zach about taking over for him."

"Consider the job yours."

My head whipped around, and I spotted Zach, Rae, and Lennix hanging on to the top of the fence.

"Thanks, buddy," I said with a laugh.

He shot me a thumbs up. "You got it." Then he waved me on. "Proceed."

Ivy and I shared a laugh as I turned to look back at her. "And I was thinkin' about mentoring some of the younger riders. The kid I helped a few weeks ago has shown some real improvement."

She reached up and cupped my cheeks, tears welling in her eyes. "You would be so good at that."

Hearing her say that meant the world to me. "You think so?"

"I know it. Because I know you. And Connor Bennett, you're a good man."

I reached into my back pocket and pulled the envelope out, holding it up between us.

"Is that . . .?"

"Our future," I answered. "Care to find out what we're havin'?"

She hopped up and down on a squeal and snatched

the envelope from my hands, ripping it open like a kid going ham on her presents Christmas morning.

She pulled out the piece of paper inside and twisted so we could read it together. A watery laugh worked its way up her throat.

"We're having a—"

CONNOR

F*ive and a half months later*

SYLVIA HAYDEN BENNETT—SYLVIE FOR SHORT—
was born at 12:03 in the morning, and the very first thing
she did the instant she came into the world was let out a
wail strong enough to rattle the walls.

Like Ivy's mom had predicted, my baby girl had a head
full of pale red hair that glowed bright beneath the flores-
cent lights of the hospital room.

As I held her clutched to my chest, staring down at her
utter perfection, my heart cracked wide open. I didn't
know it was humanly possible to love a person as much as I

loved the tiny bundle in my arms. I didn't even care that she was probably going to be as wild as her momma. In fact, I was excited to see what my little chickpea would get up to and if she could top some of the stories I'd heard about Ivy.

"She's absolutely perfect," I said in a whisper as I turned and looked at the hospital bed where my whole world laid, her hair slick with sweat and a tired smile on her beautiful face.

"She damn well better be, she made me push long enough to get her out."

Seventeen hours of labor had taken its toll on my butterfly, but she'd handled it like a champ. Even when she was screaming at me that my dick was never getting anywhere near her again.

She didn't mean it.

I was ninety-seven percent sure of that.

And if I was wrong, well, my woman couldn't resist my dimples. Or my ass. And I wasn't above fighting dirty.

My parents, along with Ivy's and all our closest friends, were currently in the waiting room waiting to meet the newest member of our family. But before I let them in, there was one last thing I needed to do.

"You want to help me give Momma her present?" I cooed down at my little monster. She blinked her eyes at me and opened her lips on a tiny yawn before passing back out. "I'll take that as a yes," I chuckled, reaching into my pocket as I moved toward the bed.

"Yay, presents!" Ivy exclaimed tiredly as I lowered to sit on the edge of the bed beside her. "It better be good. Our daughter's big-ass head is all your fault."

"Ah, but the red hair is yours."

She leaned back into the pillows with a heavy sigh. "I know. I'm already preparing for all the times I'm going to have to apologize to my mom for my childhood." She reached over and dragged her finger down our daughter's velvety cheek. "Something tells me this little one is going to give me a run for my money."

"Good thing you'll have me on your team then. Because I'm pretty sure we can handle anything just as long as we're together." I lifted the cushion-cut diamond ring, and her eyes immediately filled with tears. "What do you say, butterfly? Will you be my wife and give me more beautiful babies to drive us crazy until we're old and gray?"

"Yes!" she exclaimed on a watery laugh, wrapping her arms around my neck. "Yes, I'll marry you and give you more babies. Big-ass heads and all."

I was glad to hear it, because I intended to tangle her up with me so tightly, she'd never be able to work her way loose.

The End.

Thank you so much for reading!
Keep scrolling for a sneak peek of Hayden and Micah's story
LOVE TO HATE YOU

Want to know where Ivy got her start? Check out Hayden and Micah's story, **LOVE TO HATE YOU** now.

Prologue

Hayden

Standing in the middle of the expensive, luxurious boutique in downtown Richmond, surrounded by lace and silk and satin in every color, I felt completely and utterly ridiculous. I couldn't believe it had come to this, but desperate times called for desperate measures, and I was nothing if not painfully desperate.

"Hi. Can I help you?"

I looked up from the garment rack, the hangers holding tiny scraps of material that would barely cover my hand let alone other parts of my body. The sales clerk was a tall, svelte, modelesque blonde dressed in all black—from her sky-high heels and tight pencil skirt to her sheer silk blouse and the lacy bra beneath.

I'd never felt so frumpy in my life. I was suddenly blindingly aware that my body wasn't what it used to be back before pregnancy and childbirth changed it. I hadn't been one of those women who barely gained weight and only looked pregnant when they turned to the side. Everything from my toes to my nostrils had swelled. I'd gained more than fifty pounds while I was pregnant, and I had the stretchmarks on my stomach and breasts—even my hips—to prove it.

I lost a lot of the baby weight, but not all, and I was no

longer the slim, straight size four I'd once been. My body had permanently changed. I now had an hourglass figure. My hips were wider, my butt and chest bigger. There was no longer a gap between my thighs, and the skin around my middle was looser than it had once been.

I hadn't thought I looked bad at all, just . . . more womanly. I thought Alex would like the changes to my body, especially considering those changes came from bringing our daughter into the world. But as time passed, his interest in me seemed to be dwindling.

I could feel the distance growing between us with every passing day, and I knew I was partly to blame for it. Ivy was four now, but I'd wanted her for so long that, once she arrived, she'd become all I could see.

I'd dreamed my whole life of being a mother, and after years of trying and failing on our own *and* with medical assistance, one heartbreaking miscarriage after another, we'd finally gotten our miracle baby. Nothing mattered to me but her wellbeing, and as the years passed, I started to neglect other aspects of my life. Especially my husband.

But that was all going to change.

When I woke up this morning, I'd rolled over to find Alex's side of the bed already empty and the sheets cold. That was becoming our norm. He got up early, did his thing, and left for work without so much as a note or text.

Used to be, when things were good between us, he couldn't bring himself to leave for the day without waking me up for a goodbye kiss. Nine times out of ten, that led to hard, fast, dirty sex that left us both breathless and smiling before he inevitably forced himself to break away from me so he could head to work.

I couldn't remember the last time we'd had a day start off like that, and this morning I woke up missing it terribly. I also woke up with a fire in my belly, determined to get us back to where we used to be.

Hence the babysitter for my daughter and the high-end lingerie store for me.

I'd gotten up and actually took the time to put some care into my appearance. None of my clothes from before Ivy really fit anymore, and Alex was always making off-handed comments about me waiting until I was back to my pre-baby weight before buying anything new, so I had extremely limited wardrobe choices, but did my best. And I *thought* I'd made it work . . . until Runway Barbie showed up.

Now I was uncomfortably aware that my jeans looked —and felt—glued to my skin, and that I was currently holding them closed with a ponytail holder since I could no longer get the button anywhere near the stupid buttonhole.

"Oh, uh . . . I'm looking for something," I started lamely. "A surprise for my husband."

The woman's smile was warm and inviting. "Ah, very nice. I think I can help you find just the thing." She bounced from rack to rack, flipping through and pulling off hangers faster than I could process what was happening, all without once asking for my size.

Before I knew what was happening, I was herded toward the fitting rooms at the back of the shop. "I've grabbed some things I think would really do the trick and look fantastic on you," she said breezily as she hung my—her—selections along one of the walls. "Let me know if you need a different size in anything."

The deep red velvet dressing room curtain was slapped shut before I could manage to form a single word.

"What just happened?" I whispered to myself, slowly turning to take in the confines of the small room.

I slowly dragged the hangers back and forth, pleasantly surprised that the sales clerk had picked several pieces that were really pretty.

Stripping out of my ill-fitting clothes, I pulled one of the nighties off its hanger and tried it on. The soft silk was cool against my skin and slipped into place perfectly, proving that the clerk *really* knew her stuff.

I turned to look at myself in the long, gilded mirror. The

nightie was held in place by two thin spaghetti straps. The neckline plunged into a deep V that showed a good amount of cleavage, but the A-line actually did an incredible job of keeping my breasts in place, making them look nice and perky. The hemline didn't even reach mid-thigh, revealing a *lot* of leg, and when I turned around to check out the back, sure enough, there was more than a hint of cheek peeking out.

The light, dusky blue of the silk actually looked really nice against my pale complexion, and the peach-colored lace around the hem and bustline complemented my light red hair.

All in all, I thought I looked pretty damn good, but as I stood staring at my reflection, the determination from earlier started to flicker. I felt myself losing steam. A pep-talk was seriously needed, so I pulled my phone from my purse and hit the number on speed dial as I paced my small confines.

The phone rang and rang before voicemail finally kicked in. "Hey, honey," I spoke. "So, I know this is the third message I've left you today, but I could really use my BFF right now. Or, you know . . . whenever you're available." I blew out a sigh and looked back at myself in the mirror. "I'm currently standing in the dressing room of a lingerie store, wearing nothing but a skimpy nightie. I need you to tell me if I'm making a mistake, babe. Call me back."

My shoulders sank as I disconnected and tossed the phone back into my purse. "Well," I said to my reflection, "looks like you're in this on your own. Might as well suck it up."

I spent the next few minutes trying on the rest of the sales clerk's selections. By the time I walked out of the store half an hour later, I had four new nighties, three bra and panty sets that were a whole hell of a lot better than the stuff I'd been wearing, a new robe, and a teddy I was sure I'd never have the guts to wear but had talked myself into getting anyway. Just in case.

It wasn't often I had some free time to myself. I decided to take advantage of the beautiful day and, having a babysitter for another two hours, headed to a little bistro a couple blocks down for lunch.

As I made the short walk at a leisurely pace, I thought over my plan again. Alex's hours had been erratic over the past few months, making it so he usually didn't get home until well after the sun had gone down and I'd already put Ivy to bed. Usually I hated his late hours and going to bed alone, but I intended to make it work for me tonight.

The plan was, after getting Ivy down, I'd change into one of my newest purchases and wait in bed for my husband to come home so he could unwrap his new gift.

I was feeling good about things, hopeful even, that this would be the start of getting us back to where we once were. Pushing through the door of the bistro, I had a smile on my face and a bit of a swing in my hips as I pictured Alex's reaction.

My good mood remained in place as the hostess grabbed a menu and led the way to my table. As I followed, my attention drifted, taking in the other diners who were enjoying their meals. I came to stop in the middle of the dining area when I spotted a familiar curtain of dark brown hair at a table near the back.

Krista hadn't been answering my calls, so it felt somewhat serendipitous that I'd happen to run into my best friend on the day I needed her most. This was the perfect opportunity to show her what I'd bought. I started toward her but jerked to a halt two steps later when I spotted her lunch companion.

The arm I'd been lifting to wave slowly lowered to my side and the smile fell from my lips when I saw him lean in close and press his lips to hers in a kiss that was so *not* suitable for public.

Realization slammed into me like a wrecking ball. Everything started to make perfect sense. The pieces snapped together like a jigsaw puzzle, revealing a picture I'd been too blind to see before now. Alex's increasingly late hours, his interest in me waning until almost completely gone, the unexpected business trips out of town . . . and the fact that Krista had been avoiding me more and more over the last few months.

"Ma'am?" the hostess asked. "Are you okay?"

I absolutely wasn't.

Because I had just realized my husband and best friend were having an affair.

CLICK HERE TO KEEP READING

Jessica's Princesses

Come be a part of Jessica's Princesses Reader Group, where you'll get first looks at cover reveals, what's coming next, and so much more.

Jessica's Princesses

Born and raised around Houston, Jessica is a self proclaimed caffeine addict, connoisseur of inexpensive wine, and the worst driver in the state of Texas. In addition to being all of these things, she's first and foremost a wife and mom.

Growing up, she shared her mom and grandmother's

love of reading. But where they leaned toward murder mysteries, Jessica was obsessed with all things romance.

When she's not nose deep in her next manuscript, you can usually find her with her kindle in hand.

Connect with Jessica now

www.authorjessicaprince.com

Jessica's Princesses Reader Group

Newsletter

Instagram

Facebook

TikTok

authorjessicaprince@gmail.com

www.ingramcontent.com/pod-product-compliance
Lightning Source LLC
Chambersburg PA
CBHW061115310726
48974CB00002B/550